JOSIE'S JAZZY JOURNAL

Alexa Tewkesbury

CWR

Published 2008 by CWR, Waverley Abbey House, Waverley Lane,
Farnham, Surrey GU9 8EP, UK. Registered Charity No. 294387.
Registered Limited Company No. 1990308. Reprinted 2009, 2010.

See back of book for list of National Distributors.
Unless otherwise indicated, all Scripture references are from the
Good News Bible, copyright © American Bible Society 1966, 1971,
1976, 1992, 1994.
Concept development, editing, design and production by CWR
Illustrations: Helen Reason, Dan Donovan and CWR
Printed in Finland by WS Bookwell
ISBN: 978-1-85345-457-8

Hello! This is Josie, and I'm in the Topz Gang. If you don't know who we are, flip over to the next page and you can read all about us. ⟶

I've been one of the Gang for so long I suppose I never really think about how great it is being part of something. It's the same with Mum and Dad. I belong with them and I never think about them not being there. But when I met Gabby, I suddenly <u>had</u> to think about it. Gabby didn't feel she belonged anywhere or was part of anything. All she felt was lonely and rejected. She SO needed to know that, no matter how 'unspecial' or unlovable she might feel, God's right there waiting for her, wanting to be her friend so that she can belong to Him and be a part of **His HUGE** family.

But Gabby's a very private person, and finding ways to show her God's love turned out to be really hard.

Want to know what happened? It's all in my diary. So why not curl up and get reading!

HI! WE'RE THE TOPZ GANG

– Topz because we all live at the 'top' of something …
either in houses at the top of the hill, at the top of the
flats by the park, even sleeping in a top bunk counts!
We are all Christians, and we go to Holly Hill School.

We love Jesus, and try to work out our faith in God
in everything we do – at home, at school and with our
friends. That even means trying to show God's love to
the Dixons Gang who tend to be bullies, and can be a
real pain!

If you'd like to know more about us, visit our website
at **www.cwr.org.uk/topz** You can read all about us,
and how you can get to know and understand the Bible
more by reading our 'Topz' notes, which are great fun,
and written every two months just for you!

TUESDAY 9 FEBRUARY

Sarah rang.

'When are you going?' she asked.

'Sunday,' I said.

'When are you coming back?' she asked.

'Dunno. The following Saturday, I suppose,' I said.

'But that's the whole of half term,' Sarah moaned. 'I'm not going to see you for the whole of half term.'

She likes a good moan, Sarah does. I remember when her mum had to go away for a few days to stay with her gran because her gran had fallen over and needed lots of looking after. Phew, didn't she moan then! On and on she went. Not that I'd be very happy if <u>my</u> mum had to go away. In fact I'd be totally mizzy. But I don't think I'd have made quite such a big deal about it. People have to go away sometimes. That's the way it is. Dad has to go away with work on and off which is always a bit pooey. Mum makes it nice when he's not here, though. I get to stay up a bit later some nights and we have long chats and eat Maltesers.

So anyway, I said to Sarah, 'It'll be all right. You'll have a great half term. You'll be able to get together with John and do lots of snazzy, twin-type stuff that you don't normally do because <u>I'm</u> always here.'

Sarah said, 'Josie, if you had the faintest clue how <u>not</u> fun it is doing anything snazzy or twin-type with my brother, you'd eat your hair rather than even suggest it.'

I said, 'Eeew! Would I?'

'Yes,' she said, 'with mouldy peanut butter spread on it and everything! Can't I just come with you to the country?'

5

I said, 'Not really. Sorry.'

Of course it would be rib-tickly and wicked if Sarah <u>could</u> come – rib-tickly because we'd probably fall about laughing all the time like we usually do, and wicked because … well, it just would be – but some things you really CAN'T do. And I really CAN'T invite Sarah to the country for half term because it's not <u>her</u> Auntie Chrissie and Uncle Rich we'd be staying with. It's mine. And you can't ask other people to stay in other people's houses with you no matter how much you like them and what a groovy time you think you'd have together.

'I'll tell you all about it when I get back, though,' I said. 'I could even send you a postcard.'

Sarah said, 'If you had a mobile phone, you could text me.'

I said, 'No, I couldn't.'

She said, 'Why not?'

I said, 'Because <u>you</u> haven't got a mobile phone.'

She said, 'Well, I still think it's really mean of you to go for the whole of half term. Anyway, your aunt and uncle have got their own children. Why did they have to go and foster some other little girl?'

As soon as she said it she was sorry, though. After all, Gabby obviously needed a foster home or Auntie Chrissie and Uncle Rich wouldn't have fostered her. But she's like that, Sarah is. She gets all het up over something, then feels really bad about it. And I'm sure I'd be just as disappointed if <u>she</u> was the one going away all over half term and leaving <u>me</u> behind. I'd probably say all sorts of things I didn't mean.

Actually in some ways it's quite cool knowing someone's going to miss you if you're not around. It means they must really like you. But then Sarah and me,

U CUD TXT ME :O)

6

we're best friends and that's what best friends do – like each other, no matter how hot the oven is or what the weather's like in France. (That's what Dad says, anyway. I think he means that best friends are best friends whatever happens.)

I don't know why Auntie Chrissie and Uncle Rich decided to foster Gabby when they've already got Josh and Caley, but they did. I think they want me to go and visit because Gabby and me, we're the same age. Exactly the same. They probably hope we'll get to be good friends. Josh and Caley are older. Much older. Josh is really tall and he's got e-n-o-r-m-o-u-s feet.

WEDNESDAY 10 FEBRUARY

Sarah said, 'I've got an idea. Instead of you going to the country to stay with your Uncle Rich and Auntie Chrissie, why not ring them up and see if Gabby can come and stay here? That way you won't have to go anywhere at half term and Gabby'll get to make two friends instead of just one – you <u>and</u> me. What do you think?'

'I think it's a really good idea,' I said.

'Do you?' Sarah said. 'Do you think your Uncle Rich and Auntie Chrissie will be all right with it?'

'No,' I said.

'Why not?' Sarah said.

'I just don't think they will,' I said. 'Gabby's only been living with them for about a month. Mum says they're still trying to get to know her and she's still trying to get to know them. They want her to be all settled in – to feel that she's got a proper home now. That's why they want me to go there.'

Sarah said, 'But why will it help her to settle in if you're there? It's not as if you're going to live with them. How can you help her feel at home if it's not <u>your</u> home?'

'That's totally what I asked Mum,' I said. Honestly, it is seriously weird how Sarah and I can think exactly the same sometimes. Anyway, Mum says that if someone has been fostered by someone else it's because they haven't got a family of their own at the moment for some reason, so they need to be given the hugest amounts of love and understanding it's possible to give. She says it'll be good for Gabby to know that she's loved and cared for, not just by Auntie Chrissie and Uncle Rich (and Josh and Caley, of course), but by the WHOLE family – which includes me because of the whole cousin and being related thing.

'I suppose that what Auntie Chrissie and Uncle Rich are hoping,' I said to Sarah, 'is that me being there will help Gabby feel a part of the family – the whole family.'

'Do you think?' she said.

'Definitely,' I said.

'Mmm,' said Sarah. 'It must be horrible not having your own family. You could always tell her about God's family too. That's another family she could be part of.'

'Mmm,' I said.

'Mmm,' replied Sarah. 'Still wish you didn't have to go.'

Later

It'll be all right. Once I get there it'll be fine. I've been to stay with Auntie Chrissie and Uncle Rich before and they're really great. They keep chickens in their back garden and they've got a pond with real ducks in it, and a big sort of wire run where their guinea pigs and rabbits live. Auntie Chrissie used to want a donkey but I remember Mum saying Uncle Rich thought that would be a bit much.

I think having a donkey would be cool. I'd call it Bruno – if it was a boy, of course. If it was a girl I'm not sure what I'd call it. Sarah would come up with something good though. She's better at thinking up girls' names than I am. Then we could take turns riding it to school and it could eat the grass round the edge of the playing field all day until it was time to go home. Trouble is, we haven't got anywhere to keep a donkey. And even if we did have, Dad would probably come up with this really sensible but BORING reason why we shouldn't have one. Oh well. **Hee-haaw.**

It will be all right, though. Mum says Uncle Rich and Auntie Chrissie will spoil me rotten like they usually do.

It's just that usually when I go and stay with them, it's just me. And Josh and Caley, of course. And usually I'm only there for about two days, over a weekend or something. And usually everyone's making a big fuss of me so I don't have time to think about missing Mum and Dad too much. I do miss them anyway, though, but I know I'll be home again in the blink of an eye. This time it's different.

I said to Mum, 'Can I come home before Saturday if I want to?'

'Of course you can, silly,' said Mum. 'You can come home whenever you're ready. All Auntie Chrissie wants you to know is that you can stay till next weekend if you'd like to.'

'I think I'd like to,' I said, 'it's just ...'

'Just what?'

'What if Gabby doesn't like me? Just because I'm in her new family, it doesn't mean we're going to get on. She might hate football. She might not like playing any sort of games at all.'

Then I thought of something even worse.

'Supposing she doesn't even like climbing trees. I always climb trees when I'm at Auntie Chrissie's.'

Mum said, 'People don't have to like exactly the same things to get on with each other. The most important thing for Gabby to realise is that she's part of a new family who all want to get to know her and help her feel welcome and wanted.'

'But what if I don't make her feel any of those things?' I said.

'You will,' said Mum. 'I know you will. When you go to bed tonight, ask God to give you all the love you'll need to love Gabby and that's what He'll give you – all the love you'll need. Every last drop.'

In bed

I've never thought of love coming in drops. Good idea, though. I think I'm going to picture myself as a dropper bottle when I go away – like one of those little plastic squeezy ones I got from the doctor when I had an ear infection. Mum had to put the end bit down inside my ear while I lay on my side on the bed, and then squeeze out a little dribble. It tickled like crazy when it ran down inside my ear and it was dead cold because the bottle had to be kept in the fridge. Only God's love isn't freezing like that – it's warm, and it's not tickly, it's comforting. So maybe being a dropper bottle isn't such a good idea.

What I really need to be is a watering can! That way I can SHOWER Gabby with God's love all the time. I'll just have to remember to keep asking Him to top me up.

It will be all right at Auntie Chrissie's. It <u>will be all right</u>.

I'm just a bit scared though.

I wonder what Gabby's short for?

THURSDAY 11 FEBRUARY
Cool! Coool! COOOOOOOOOOL!!

Mrs Parker says she's starting up an after school drama club on Wednesdays after half term! Totally brilliant or what?!

FRIDAY 12 FEBRUARY

Sarah reckons Mrs Parker should make the after school drama club into a proper theatre group and call it something like The Holly Hill Theatre Company.

Then she said, 'Actually, now I come to think of it, The Holly Hill Theatre Company is a bit of a boring name, isn't it? What about … The Holly Hill Hoppers?'

I pointed out that calling it the something or other 'Hoppers' made it sound more like a dance company, so she had another think, then said, 'I know! The Hilly Hollies! We could be called The Hilly Hollies and we could practise plays and go touring all round lots of different schools performing them.'

'Could we?' I said.

'Yes!' she said. 'And we could have programmes with all our names in and pictures of hills and holly leaves on the covers.'

'Could we?' I said.

'We could,' she said.

Sarah often gets very excited about things. She sometimes has some of her best ideas when she's excited. I'm not sure about the touring theatre company, though. I thought we probably needed to look a bit on the sensible side.

'I suppose we could,' I said (sensibly), 'but the club hasn't even started yet and we don't know what Mrs Parker will want to do.'

'I know <u>that</u>,' Sarah said, giving me her best 'why do you always have to be so sensible?' look, 'but if she asks for suggestions, we want to be ready with some really fantastic ones, don't we?'

Good point. Nothing like being prepared, I suppose.

'And that's another thing,' Sarah said. 'I've been thinking.'

'What about?' I asked.

'About Gabby,' she said.

'And?' I said. 'I'm sorry but you still can't come with me.'

'I know I can't,' she said.

'No, what I was thinking was that you <u>could</u> still sort of take me. Only it wouldn't actually be me, of course.'

'Sarah, what on earth are you talking about?'

'We could write a character profile for me.'

'A what?'

'A character profile,' Sarah said. 'Famous people have them on the internet and places. There's a photograph and then all sorts of information about them – when they were born, where they live, their favourite food, what they like doing. We can write all that sort of stuff down about me and make it into a booklet or something, and I'm sure Mum and Dad have got a photo we could stick on. Then you can give it to Gabby and she'll know all about me, even what I look like. She can get to know me from reading my profile. It'll be sort of like me coming with you.'

Like I say, Sarah definitely does have some of her best ideas when she's excited. A profile is a wicked idea! Not only does it mean that Gabby can read all about my best friend, it also means that she'll feel even more welcome because my best friend bothered to put a profile together for her. Then maybe Gabby will want to write her own for Sarah to read when I get home.

Gabby and Sarah can be like kind of 'profile pals'! And when they eventually meet up, which I'm sure they will, they'll get on really well because in a way they'll have already met.

I noticed that Sarah's mouth had suddenly dropped open and her eyes had gone all big and staring.

'What is it?' I said.

'I've had a **QUADRUPLE BRILLY** idea!' she beamed.

'Another one?' I said. It's hard to believe someone could have so many quadruple brilly ideas in such a short space of time.

'Yes! We could do a profile of God, too! That way, when you want to talk to Gabby about Him, you can just whip out His profile and let her read it. We can put in how loving He is, and how much He wants to be friends with her, and how all the angels would get together and have a huge party if she decided to ask Him to be part of her life because then she'd be one of His family!'

It can be quite humbling to have a friend who's so full of good ideas. Sarah says it's usually me who comes up with all the fandabby-whatsit stuff, but I think I must be having a pretty bad day from an ideas point of view, not having had ANY so far.

Still, we've got plenty to keep us going with all of Sarah's. She's coming round tomorrow morning so we can get writing. Mum says busy brains like Sarah's need feeding. She's making trifle.

SATURDAY 13 FEBRUARY — HALF TERM

YESSSS!!

Sarah was here for ages. I think she may have had <u>three</u> bowls of trifle – with ice cream. Her brain was obviously very hungry.

When her dad came and picked her up, Mum said, 'Sarah may not want any lunch.'

Mind you, we worked mega hard. There's a lot to think about when you're doing character profiles. Loads actually.

Sarah's profile goes like this:

ALL ABOUT SARAH

(We stuck a photo of her here. She's wearing her cycle helmet but she looks very happy, so Sarah thought it would be a good one to use.)

NAME: Sarah
EYE COLOUR: Blue
HAIR COLOUR: Blonde
BEST FRIEND: Josie
BROTHER: One called John who also happens to be my twin.
PETS: One cat called Saucy, and John has a dog called Gruff.
MOST ANNOYING THING: John
SCHOOL: Holly Hill
FAVE FOOD: Puddings like trifle and ice cream and treacle tart.

FAVE COLOUR: Sometimes pink, but then again not always.

FAVE STUFF: Being God's friend, being in the Topz Gang, going to Sunday Club, learning keyboards, singing, cuddly animals, messing about with Josie, old people because they can be your favourite people too.

UN-FAVE STUFF: Homework, people walking into my bedroom without knocking first (ie John), getting up early, the Dixons Gang (because they can be really mean to us Topz when we haven't done anything to them at all), the dark.

MOST WANT TO: Meet up with you and make friends.

I wasn't sure about that last 'MOST WANT TO' bit. I didn't want it to sound too pushy. I said to Sarah that, for all we know, Gabby is really shy and will find it difficult making friends with people who are actually <u>in</u> her own new family let alone with people who aren't, even if they are incredibly friendly and kind and all that, like Sarah.

Sarah said, 'I think Gabby ought to know I'd like to meet her though. I'd be really pleased if I thought someone was interested enough to want to meet me. Wouldn't you?'

'I suppose I would now you put it like that,' I said. 'But maybe we could add, "Only if you want to, of course." That would show we're thinking about what Gabby might want as well.'

So that's what we did.

When we'd finished Sarah's profile, we had a trifle and ice cream break. In fact we had two trifle and ice cream breaks one after the other without a gap, mostly because we felt that our brains needed an extra special boost before we sat down to work out a profile for God. It suddenly seemed like a very huge and important thing to do. And we had to get it absolutely right. You see, Gabby needs to know EXACTLY how much God loves her.

It took ages and we changed it loads but in the end this is what we wrote. We think it's got all the important bits now:

THIS IS GOD

(No photo, obviously.)

NAMES: God, Lord, Father.
AGE: Ageless. He's always been here and always will be.
JOB: Creator of everything and He loves all that He's made.
CHILDREN: One Son called Jesus who came to earth to live with us and to teach us about Him and how to be His friend, but He wants all people on earth to become His children too. (That'd be too many names to write down, though).
FAVE STUFF: He knows everything there is to know about us and wants us to get to know Him as well. He loves loving us, listening to us when we talk to Him, helping us when we're in trouble, comforting us when we're upset, being a friend to us when we're lonely, just being close to us always. He also likes it when we do these things for each other. He's especially happy when someone new wants to be His friend because He wants all people to know Him so that He can be with them forever.

> **UN-FAVE STUFF:** When people are unkind to each other, or selfish, or mean, or jealous, or tell lies, or do other nasty things that He doesn't want us to do. (He still loves us when we do these things, but He doesn't like the nasty things we sometimes do.) It also makes Him sad when people ignore Him and don't want to get to know Him because, after all, He made us and is our Father in heaven.

When we'd finished, FINALLY it was me who had a good idea.

I said, 'I'm not going to Gabby's till tomorrow afternoon. We could always show Louise what we've written in the morning at Sunday Club. Leaders like it when you ask them about stuff like this. Then we'd still have time to change anything or add bits if she thought we'd left out something vitally important.'

'Brilliant idea!' said Sarah. 'Can I scrape out the trifle dish?'

In bed

Did all my packing with Mum. She said I had to put in lots of changes of everything because she didn't know how wet and muddy I might get (what with it being a cold, rainy February and there being heaps of mud in the country), and she didn't want Auntie Chrissie to be stuck with piles of washing.

I said, 'It'll be all right, won't it, me staying there?'

Mum said, 'Of course it'll be all right. I think you're going to have a wonderful time.'

I asked, 'Will you ring me every day?'

Mum said, 'Definitely. Probably more than once.'

I asked, 'Do you think you'll miss me?'

Mum said, 'You have no idea how much.'

I wonder if Mum and Dad will miss me as much as I'm going to miss them. I want to go and meet Gabby, I do, honestly, it's just it's almost a whole week. I know I can come home in the middle if I want to, but I shouldn't really. I should stay and make friends with her. I should stay because she needs to know that she belongs to a whole new family. I should stay. I mean, it's exciting. It's just … it's almost a whole week …

SUNDAY 14 FEBRUARY

I'm getting up now. Bye-bye bed. See you in almost a whole week.

NEARLY TIME TO GO!
Just checking round my room to see if I've forgotten anything. I don't think I have. Anyway, Dad says if I do forget something I'll be gone for such a short time I'll hardly have a moment to miss it. He's probably right – except if the forgotten thing is something like my toothbrush, I suppose. Although, would I really miss not brushing my teeth for almost a whole week? (Bleeahh! I think I might actually.)

I wasn't going to take my diary with me. I thought it might seem a bit rude to keep disappearing off to write down everything that's going on. Only Sarah said I had to take it. She said how else would I remember everything I did with Gabby and everything we talked about if I didn't write it all down – given that I'd need to tell Sarah EVERY detail when I got home again, of course.

I'm going to miss Sarah SO much. Oodles and oodles. It was horrible saying goodbye after Sunday Club.

I said, 'This is horrible! I'm going to miss you SO much!'

Sarah said, 'I'm going to miss you so much too.'

John said, 'How can you possibly be going to miss Josie when you get to spend the whole of half term with me?'

Sarah said, 'Do you really want me to answer that?'

I think even Benny and Paul looked a bit sad, and Danny said it'd be funny meeting up for Topz Rules footie and me not being there.

'Still,' he said, 'it's not for long, is it?'

'It is, actually,' I said. 'It's almost a whole week.'

'I know,' he said, 'but that's not really, really long.'

Yes it is, I thought. It's almost a whole week …

(Louise loved our character profile of God, by the way. She said she wouldn't change a single thing. She's going to pray for Gabby to come to know God exactly the way Sarah and I do. That's what I'm going to pray, too.)

Dad says it's time to go. I haven't forgotten my toothbrush. And I'm not forgetting my diary. It's going in the top of my bag. Right now.

Gabby's bedroom

I'm here. Mum and Dad have gone home. I've unpacked my stuff. Gabby's gone to watch TV. I've got to go down in a minute.

It's so awkward, though. Auntie Chrissie and Uncle Rich gave me a huge hug and so did Josh and Caley. They all went on for ages about how much I'd grown since they last saw me (funny how people do that – I mean, it's not as if I'm going to have got smaller, is it?) and did I still enjoy playing football and all that stuff.

But, Gabby and me, we just sort of looked at each other. We didn't know what to say. She didn't even smile at me, not really. Auntie Chrissie says not to worry and it'll just take a little time for Gabby to get used to having me here. But I don't think she likes me. We're sharing a bedroom but I don't think she wants to. I don't think this is going to work out. I don't think we'll get on.

I wish Sarah was here.

I want to go home.

Bedtime

I was in bed first. Gabby was still having her bath. She must be a really quiet person because she came in while I had my diary out and I never heard a thing. I closed it ever so quickly and went to slide it into my bag. I didn't really want her to know about it. But it was too late. She'd already seen it.

Gabby said, 'What have you got there?'
I said, 'It's nothing. Not really. It's just … my diary.'
Gabby said, 'Oh, you keep a diary, do you?'
'Yes,' I said (only please don't ask if you can read it!).
Gabby didn't ask if she could read it.
She said, 'That's funny. So do I.'

MONDAY 15 FEBRUARY

Gabby keeps a diary! That is just SO cool! I can't wait to tell Sarah. I mean, if Gabby keeps a diary like us, there are probably other things she does like us. Maybe she even likes climbing trees.

Breakfast's ready. I can smell toast.

Later

Mum rang.

I said, 'You'll never guess where I've just been!'

She said, 'To the moon on a bicycle?'

I said, **'NO! IN A TREE HOUSE!**

'Uncle Rich has built Gabby a tree house in their orchard. So she's got a special place to go, or something. It's got a ladder up to it and everything, but Gabby doesn't use the ladder. She says ladders are for people with the climbing skills of an ostrich. She just gets up there using the branches. That's what I did too, and she said my climbing skills were obviously far superior to any ostrich she'd ever seen. AND Gabby keeps a diary. Just like me and Sarah!'

Mum said, 'But Gabby is just like you and Sarah. So you're having a good time, then?'

I said, 'And guess what I had for breakfast?'

Mum said, 'Fried egg on doughnuts?'

'No!' I said. 'Toast. But not ordinary toast. Auntie Chrissie makes the bread and I had homemade honey on it.'

'Homemade honey?' Mum said.

'Yes,' I said. 'They've got their own bees now. I mean, just imagine having your own bees.'

Mum said, 'Is everything all right, though?'

I didn't answer straightaway.

I wanted to say, 'Not exactly. I miss you, Mum. Gabby and me, we like some of the same sort of stuff, but we still don't really know what to say to each other.'

I wanted to say, 'She showed me the tree house but I don't think she really wanted to. It's her special place, you see, no one else's.'

I wanted to say, 'I'd sort of like to come home now. I'm sure Gabby's really nice but she's not all chatty with me like I thought she might be. And I don't feel all chatty with her like I thought I would. And I haven't told her about Sarah because I don't know if she's got any friends here and she might think it's not fair that

I've got friends <u>and</u> my very own family.'

I couldn't, though. I couldn't say any of it. I was on the phone in the kitchen and Auntie Chrissie and Caley were in there. It would have been unkind to say I was unhappy when they were trying so hard to make me feel at home. So I didn't. I made out I was all whoop-de-doo and cheerful.

'Yes, Mum,' I said. 'Everything's fine.'

But Mum knew. She knew inside me everything wasn't fine. That's what mums do, isn't it? They know stuff like that about you.

She said, 'Auntie Chrissie's not going to mind if you don't want to stay until Saturday, Josie.'

'I know,' I said. 'I'm fine, though. Will you ring me later?'

'Try and stop me,' Mum said. 'Love you.'

'I love you too, Mum.'

I put the phone down.

That's when I saw Gabby. She was staring at me. She'd heard me say that. 'I love you.' And all of a sudden I realised. Gabby hasn't got a mum to know stuff about her. She hasn't got anyone to say, 'I love you' to. And she hasn't got anyone to say, 'I love you' to her. Not someone of her very own. Not like I've got.

So I decided. Right there and then. I've got to stay. I'm sure God wants me to stay. He wants us to help people who are lonely, not leave them. God would never leave someone who's lonely.

I've got to stay

Dear Father, I'm sorry I feel sad. I've got nothing to feel sad about. I really miss Mum and Dad but please help me to remember that at least I have a mum and dad to go home to. Poor Gabby hasn't. I know she's got Uncle Rich and Auntie Chrissie now, but it can't be the same. It can't be like having your own mum and dad who know you upside down and right side up and love you to absolute bits. At least that's what it's like with <u>my</u> mum and dad. And that's what it's like with You, too, isn't it? Please help me to show Gabby who You are so that she can have You as her friend and Father in heaven. Help me to explain that she doesn't need to feel lonely because You'll never leave her. Help me to think about what it's like for Gabby to be here and not what it's like for me. And help me to show her Your love. Amen.

Bedtime

Gabby and me, we're writing our diaries.

We were in the tree house earlier.

I said to Gabby, 'Are you sure you don't mind if I'm in here?'

She said, 'Why would I mind? It's not like it's mine or anything.'

'It is yours, though,' I said. 'Uncle Rich and Josh built it for you.'

'Maybe,' she shrugged. 'But when I'm not here any more, it'll be someone else's, won't it?'

'What do you mean?' I said. 'Why wouldn't you be here any more?'

'This is only a foster home, isn't it?' she said. 'A person can have loads of different foster homes.'

'But I thought Uncle Rich and Auntie Chrissie want you to stay with them.'

'So they say. But you never can tell, can you? That's what Rose says.'

'Who's Rose?' I asked.

'She was in the children's home,' Gabby said. 'You know, where I was before I came here. Only of course you don't know, do you, because you live with your mum and dad, so why would you?'

'So, Rose is your friend?' I asked. I felt so uncomfortable I didn't really know what to say at all.

'Oh no,' Gabby said. 'Rose says there's no point having friends when you're in care. She says you get moved around so much that friendships are pointless and a waste of time because you can't keep them anyway. And she says you should never think of a foster place as your home because at any moment you could be told you've got to leave. It happens to her all the time. Rose says you can't trust anyone.'

'But,' I said, 'but maybe Rose has never been fostered by anyone like Auntie Chrissie and Uncle Rich. Just because she's had to move around a lot, it doesn't mean you're going to have to.'

'And how would you know?' Gabby said.

'I just do,' I said. 'I know they really want you to be here.'

'Anyway,' she said, 'I'll probably be able to go back to my own home soon. Dad'll come and take me there and everything'll be fine. I won't even need a foster family.'

I couldn't make it out. If Gabby had her own dad, why was she here at all?

She must have seen it all over my face because she said, 'You didn't know I had a dad, did you? Well, of course I've got a dad. I'm not a sad little orphan. My mum's not here. She was ill and now she's just … not here. I've got a dad, though. I'm not so different from you. Dad was going to look after me only he didn't seem to be able to. For some reason. That's why I had to go to the children's home last year. He's going to come for me, though. He really misses me. And when he misses me enough he's going to come for me.'

It's the saddest thing I've ever heard – no mum; a dad somewhere or other but you don't know where he is or when you'll get to see him again; and having to live with people you don't trust because someone's told you not to trust anyone.

Gabby stopped talking. There was this silence. I'm sure she was waiting for me to say something.

All I could think of was, 'We can still be friends though, can't we?' Stupid. How could being friends with me possibly make up for everything Gabby didn't have?

'I told you,' she said. 'I don't make friends. Anyway, you'll be gone in a few days.'

'But while I'm here,' I said. 'Can't we be friends while I'm here?'

She looked at me and screwed her mouth up in a funny way.

'We can do stuff together,' she said, 'because you're here and I'm here and that's what happens when you're with someone. You do stuff together. You're not my friend, though.'

And that was it. All weird and strange and sad and lonely. And Gabby, well, I think she must be the loneliest person I've ever met.

TUESDAY 16 FEBRUARY

Awake really early. The bedroom was pitch black. I wasn't even sure where the window was. There don't seem to be any streetlights in the country.

I'm sure Gabby was crying. I'm sure that's why I woke up. I asked her if she was all right and she said, yes, of course she was.

I said, 'Sorry. It's just … I thought I heard you crying.'

She said, 'Why would I be crying? I was asleep. You woke me up.'

I didn't wake her up. She wasn't asleep. I know she was crying.

Nearly lunch

After breakfast Caley said, 'I'm walking down to the village shop in a minute. Who wants to come?'

I looked at Gabby. She shook her head.

She said, 'You can go if you want to.'

I said, 'Are you sure you don't mind?'

She said, 'You don't have to keep asking me if I mind. It's up to you what you do.'

I was glad it was just me and Caley in the end. Not in a nasty way, I just really wanted a chat. Caley and I have good chats when I visit.

I said, 'I keep saying the wrong thing to Gabby.'

Caley said, 'No, you don't. Gabby's like that with all of us. It's hard for her. It's her first foster home so it must be really strange.'

'You all want her to stay here, though, don't you?' I said.

'Of course we do,' said Caley. 'Why?'

'Gabby doesn't seem to think so. She told me. And I heard her crying in the night.'

'I think she cries most nights.'

'Will her dad come back?' I asked.

Caley just shrugged her shoulders.

'What about your church?' I said. 'Has she been there with you?'

'No,' Caley said. 'She won't come. Mum says we can't force her and she'll come when she's ready.'

'The thing is,' I said, 'I was going to try and talk to her about God. I wanted her to know that however lonely she feels, actually she's never on her own at all because He's always there. Sarah and I had it all worked out. But then Gabby said all this stuff to me about not having friends and not trusting anyone and I thought, how can I explain it to her? If she can't even trust people, how's she ever going to understand about trusting God?'

Caley says that for now I shouldn't think too much about everything and just try to be me. She says that the more normal and ordinary things are, the better it is for Gabby. She says I should talk about whatever comes into my head – my life at home, my friends, my school.

'It should be easier for you than for me because you're the same age,' Caley said. 'I think that's why Mum hoped you'd come. You'd be sort of like a ready-made friend. Gabby may pretend she doesn't want to know anything about you, but underneath I bet she really does. I bet she just wants to be normal like us.'

Normal, I thought. Am I normal?

Sarah would probably say, **'You? Normal? You're about as normal as a coconut in a cabbage patch.'**

Then I'd probably say, **'Well, you're about as normal as a caterpillar wearing wellies.'**

Then Sarah would probably say, **'Well, you're about as normal as a fish on a trampoline.'**

Then I'd probably say, **'Well, you're about as normal as ... Benny!'**

And then Sarah would probably give me a shove, and I'd probably pretend to fall over and then we'd both end up in a wriggly heap on the floor and not be able to stop laughing for about the next three days.

I wish it could be like that with Gabby. Please, Lord God, please let it get to be like that with Gabby.

(Gabby came in while I was writing this.

She said, 'You spend more time writing in that thing than I spend writing in mine.'

I said, 'Do I?'

She said, 'Yes, you do, actually.'

I said, 'Oh. Do you mind?'

She said, 'Don't start that again. And by the way, lunch is ready.')

After lunch

Just written a postcard to Sarah. It's got a picture of two brown cows looking over a gate. I bought it in the shop this morning. I wrote:

Dear Sarah,

I'm having a muddy time in the country. Gabby has a tree house which is wicked but a bit cold and draughty at the moment as it's February. She keeps a diary, too. We don't spend all our time laughing like you and me. Going horseriding this afternoon because Josh has a job at this stable up the road. Dead nervous, though. I've only ever been on a donkey before. At the beach. I fell off.

Lots of love Josie

P.S. Miss you loads. Tee hee. XXXXX

I told Gabby about the falling off the donkey thing.

She said, 'Did you hurt yourself?'

I said, 'Not really, but it must have looked pretty funny.'

Gabby said, 'Did anyone laugh?'

I said, 'No. But my friend, Sarah, would have done if she'd been there. She always laughs at stuff like that.'

Gabby said, 'Doesn't sound like much of a friend if she laughs at you.'

'No, it's good,' I said. 'We always laugh at each other. She laughs when I fall off my bike, too.'

'You fall off your bike?' Gabby said in a kind of 'how could anyone be so stupid as to fall off their bike?' way.

'Oh, yeah,' I said. 'All the time. Sometimes you can't see my knees for all the scrapes and bruises.'

(This was our first proper conversation – you know, an actual buddy buddy, chatty one – and it was going REALLY well.)

Gabby said, 'You're a bit of a loon, aren't you?'

I said, 'Definitely. But ever so normal, though.'

Back from horseriding

Waiting for the shower. I said Gabby could go first because she's so much muddier than I am. She says she isn't but she SO is because:

number 1,

I managed not to fall off my horse and

number 2,

I'm not the one who jumped off my horse into this really squelchy bit of the field. Mud splatted up everywhere! Gabby even got this big dollop on her nose. I laughed. I tried not to but I couldn't help it.

Only, then I saw the expression on Gabby's face. It wasn't exactly happy.

I thought, **oh no!** I shouldn't have done that.

But, guess what? All of a sudden she started laughing, too. And there we were, up to our knees in mud (well, almost) in the middle of a field totally killing ourselves. It was SO cool. Absolutely the best. Totally hilariously MEGA in fact. Loved it!

MEGA
loved it!

In bed

When we got our diaries out Gabby said, 'Are you going to write absolutely pages and pages like you did yesterday?'

'I don't know,' I said. 'I never know how much I'm going to write until I start.'

She said, 'Are you writing about me?'

Oh dear, I thought, supposing she doesn't want me to.

'Well … yes … a bit,' I said. 'I mean, I am staying here with you so I've sort of got to, haven't I, because you're the person I'm with. Is that all right?'

'It's not up to me what you write about, is it?' said Gabby. 'Anyway, I'm writing about you.'

'Are you?' I said. I was quite pleased actually.

'Yes,' said Gabby. 'I've just put, "Josie's still here. I thought she'd have gone home by now."'

I wasn't sure what to say. I didn't know if she was joking. She wasn't.

'Why did you think I'd have gone home?' I said.

She did the screwy-up mouth thing. 'I just thought you would. I could see you were missing your family. It's not as if you <u>have</u> to stay here, is it? Not like me.'

'But I want to. I really want us to be friends.'

'What for?' she said. 'You've got friends. You've got that Sarah girl for a start.'

'I know,' I said, 'but I'd still like to be friends with you.'

Then suddenly Gabby said, 'What's she like then, this Sarah girl? Apart from laughing at you all the time. I bet she's nothing like me.'

(I wasn't sure about Gabby calling her 'this Sarah girl'. It sounded as though she didn't like Sarah. But how can you not like someone you haven't even met? I thought, it must just be the way Gabby says things.)

This Sarah girl!!

HMMM

Folded up in the back of my diary were the character profiles I'd brought – the one of Sarah and the one of God. I'd begun to think I'd never be able to show them to Gabby. She wasn't friendly that way. I could imagine her saying, 'Haven't you got anything better to do with your friends than write down this character rubbish? How tragic.' I still don't know if I can show her the one of God. I don't know if I'm brave enough. Only sometimes you need to be brave. That's what Louise says at Sunday Club. She says, 'Why wouldn't you tell people about God? Why would you keep something so amazing and wonderful to yourself?'

'If you really want to know what Sarah's like,' I said slowly, 'I can sort of show you.'

Then I handed her Sarah's profile.

'What's this?' Gabby said.

'Sarah wrote it for you,' I said. 'We did it together. Sarah thought it would be a way for you to get to know her a bit. She'd really like to meet you, you see.'

Gabby sat staring at me for a moment. She didn't say anything. She just stared. Then she unfolded the paper.

For some reason, I started smiling. I could feel this grin beginning to spread itself all over my face. Gabby was reading about Sarah! She was looking at her photo. That meant she was finding out about one of my friends; which meant she was getting to know a bit about my life at home; which meant she'd see that Sarah's one of God's friends and discover we're in the Topz Gang; and she'd be bound to ask what the Topz Gang was all about which meant I'd be able to tell her what we do and where we go, and about God being her

38

Topz Gang

Father in heaven and wanting to love her and be close to her so that she wouldn't have to feel so lonely and unwanted. Because she does. She feels SO unwanted. That's why she says I can't be her friend. She thinks I'm going to up and leave her and not want to know anymore. Just like Rose said.

Only in the end it wasn't like that. It wasn't like that at all. Gabby only glanced at the profile for a moment. Then suddenly she was staring at me again. I must have looked like such a sad little loser with that stupid grin all over my stupid face.

'Nope.' That's what Gabby said. 'I knew it. This Sarah girl's nothing like me.'

And she dropped the profile on the floor. It fell face down. All our work. All our effort. Gabby just dropped it on the floor. When she lay down in bed, she turned her back on me.

I was really, really quiet when I leaned over to pick it up. I didn't want Gabby to look at me. I didn't want her to watch me slide it back into my diary. I didn't want her to know I was hugging my diary with Sarah's photo in harder than I've ever hugged anything. It was the only way I could try and say sorry to Sarah because, even though Sarah didn't know what Gabby had done, I knew – and it really hurt me.

And another thing. I didn't want Gabby to see I was crying.

WEDNESDAY 17 FEBRUARY

I said to Auntie Chrissie after breakfast, 'Please can I go upstairs and phone Mum?'

'Of course you can,' she said.

I went up to Uncle Rich's study but I'd only just shut the door when Auntie Chrissie came in after me.

'What's the matter?' she asked. 'Has something happened with Gabby?'

I could have tried to say, 'No, nothing's happened,' I suppose. I didn't want to talk about it with Auntie

Chrissie. I didn't want her to know. All I wanted to do was say to Mum, 'Can you come and get me? **Today. As soon as possible. Now even.'**

Only, of course, Auntie Chrissie knew there was something up. She couldn't <u>not</u> know. My eyes were still all red and swollen from crying in the night. I'd splashed loads of cold water on them when I got up but it hadn't made the tiniest bit of difference. I still looked like a blubby-eyed freak.

That's probably what Gabby would have called me if she'd bothered to say anything to me at all.

She'd have said, 'What's up with you, you blubby-eyed freak?'

Except that she didn't. She ignored me. She didn't say anything when she got up. She didn't say anything at breakfast. I don't even know where she is. I think she might be in the tree house.

So that's when I decided to tell Auntie Chrissie all about it. The more I thought about what Gabby had done, the angrier I got. I didn't care if she got in trouble. I think I wanted her to.

I said, 'How could she do that? How could she throw my best friend's character profile on the floor? It's as if she threw Sarah on the floor. She doesn't even know Sarah. Sarah's never done anything to her. And neither have I.'

I waited for it. You know, all the usual telling-off stuff grown-ups come out with: 'What an ungrateful, unkind girl that Gabby is. She should be ashamed of herself. And after you've been so kind to her as well. I'm going to give her a piece of my mind right now.' It's what I wanted Auntie Chrissie to say. After all, Gabby deserved it.

But Auntie Chrissie didn't say any of that.

Instead she said, 'I'm sorry.'

I thought, why are <u>you</u> sorry? You haven't done anything. It's her. It's that Gabby girl. Gobby Gabby I think I'll call her.

Auntie Chrissie said, 'Gabby so needs to know she's not on her own. That's why I thought it would be good for her to have you here for a few days – someone her own age she could make friends with. She needs to know that there are people around her who care about her.'

'She doesn't, though,' I said. 'She doesn't want anyone to care about her. She won't <u>let</u> anyone care about her.'

'That's because she's afraid,' Auntie Chrissie said. 'All Gabby knows is that she used to have a home and a family of her own and now she hasn't got them any more. She feels so rejected.'

I was getting even crosser now. 'If Gabby feels rejected then she knows how horrible it is. So why would she reject someone else? Because that's what she's done to Sarah and me, isn't it? She's rejected us. And it's SO mean and SO unfair!'

'I know,' said Auntie Chrissie. She seemed very sad when she said it, too. 'It is mean and unfair. But the trouble is, rejection is all Gabby knows at the moment. How you're feeling today is how Gabby must feel all the time.'

What was she talking about? Was I supposed to care how Gabby feels after what she'd done to me?

'If Gabby trusts us,' Auntie Chrissie went on, 'if she lets herself be one of the family and be your friend, as far as she can see, she's going to risk that rejection all over again.'

'But why? It's not as if we're going to leave her, is it?'

'No, we're not. How does Gabby get to believe that, though – when everyone's left her before?'

I don't know what it was. Maybe it was the way Auntie Chrissie explained it. I could sort of see what she meant, though. I mean, if you know what it's like to be rejected, I suppose it must hurt so badly you'd do anything not to let it happen again. And the best way Gabby could think of to avoid being rejected again was to shut everyone out. Which is exactly what she was doing.

It's what I wanted to do, too. The best way not to let Gabby hurt me again was to shut her out – by going home.

HOME

Later

Had a long chat with Mum on the phone. She said of course she'd come and get me today if that's what I really wanted, but maybe how I was feeling would pass and would I like to stay for a bit longer and see how I felt at the end of the day.

I said, 'It's not going to pass. Gabby doesn't want to know me. She doesn't want to know anything about me. I think I can understand why now but that doesn't make me feel any better about it.'

Then Mum said (all of a sudden and out of the blue and I really wasn't sure why), 'Jesus was rejected, wasn't He?'

'I don't know,' I said. 'I suppose so.' (As if that had anything to do with it anyway.)

'Of course He was,' Mum said. 'He's God's Son and He came to earth to bring God's love and forgiveness for all the things we've done wrong. He came to bring us a whole new life, but we rejected Him. We sent Him to die a horrible death on a cross because we didn't like the things He said.'

So? I thought. What's that got to do with me staying here another day?

'Only, when we rejected Jesus,' Mum went on, 'He didn't turn round and say to God, "Do you know what, I can't be bothered with this lot any more. Look at them. They're so ungrateful. They've really hurt Me. I'm glad I'm getting out of here. I'm not having anything to do with them ever again." Jesus didn't say that, did He?'

No, I thought, but that's not what I'm saying either. I'm not saying I never want anything to do with Gabby again. I just don't feel like being <u>here</u> any more.

'Jesus did the exact opposite of what you'd think He might do, ' Mum said. 'He asked God to forgive everyone. And even though people still reject Him now, all these years later, every day, by ignoring Him or not wanting to listen to what He has to say, or just by not thinking about Him, He still doesn't reject us. He carries on praying for us. He keeps loving us. He hangs on to us for all He's worth. And He'll never give up on us. Not ever.'

There's only one thing worse than <u>not</u> being able to understand something – and that's being able to understand something you really didn't want to have to understand. Right at that minute, I SO didn't want to understand how Jesus keeps on loving us and sticks with us no matter how much we let Him down or push Him out. I SO didn't want to understand that the best way I could help Gabby was to stay with her and keep on being her friend even though I felt as if she'd thrown me and Sarah in the dustbin, slammed the lid down and then sat on it. I SO didn't want to understand that I somehow had to find a way to tell Gabby that there's a huge, enormous, FANTASTIC God out there who just wants to love her and will never let her down.

But I did understand. I knew exactly what Mum was talking about. And I had to forget all about what <u>I</u> wanted and think about what Gabby needs.

And, dear Lord God, I'm so sorry, I really am SO sorry I called her Gobby Gabby.

Nearly supper
Gabby just caught me. I was trying to scribble in here quickly without her knowing. She thinks I'm weird as it is with the amount of stuff I write. She doesn't seem to put much in her diary at all. Mind you, she doesn't have a best friend waiting for her who's going to want to know the total, complete and

ABSOLUTE FULL STORY

of my trip to the country like I have (ie Sarah – not that I want Sarah to know about the character profile being dropped on the floor bit).

I thought, Gabby's watching TV and supper's not for five minutes, that'll just give me time to write 'Still here. Decided not to go home today after all. Had a really cool afternoon, too.' Wrong. I dashed upstairs, sat on the bed, opened my diary and in came Gabby. I don't mind that she came in. I mean, it's her bedroom, how can I mind?

It's just that she said, 'Still writing about me, then?'

I said, 'No. Well, yes. But only about how clever you are and how amazing you've made your jeans look by sewing all those little buttons on them.'

That's what we've been doing this afternoon, you see. It was pouring with rain, and we were going to go out for a cycle ride with Josh, only Auntie Chrissie said, no, it was just too yucky. So after lunch she got out all these buttons, loads and loads of them, that she'd picked up at the recycling centre. Some of them were really gorgeous, too – tiny and pearly, and bright orange with little wavy edges. She said why didn't we use them to personalise some of our clothes. So I sewed some onto my jeans and some onto my hoodie in sort of swirly patterns, and Gabby sewed lots of teeny tiny ones onto her jeans down the front of the legs and they looked SO cool.

I said, 'My stuff just looks as if I've been randomly covering it with buttons, but yours looks really artistic.'

'You think?' she said.

'Yes, I do think,' I said.

'Shows what you know about art, then, doesn't it?' she said, and went back downstairs.

It hasn't upset me, though, her saying that. I don't think she meant it nastily. I think it's just her way of telling me, 'Don't be nice to me. It makes it harder for me not to be nice to you.'

I'm sticking with it, though. If Jesus can stick with us after everything we did to Him, I've got to be able to stick with Gabby.

MY PRAYER EARLIER TODAY:

Dear Lord, I'm sorry for being angry with Gabby. It was only because she hurt my feelings. I didn't understand how she could do what she did. But then, she doesn't understand what's been done to her either. Lord God, if possible, please help us to understand each other better from now on. Help Gabby to see that I'm not going to be here and gone like she thinks I am. And help me not to get hurt by what she says and the way she says it. And, most important of all, please help me to be brave enough to show her Your character profile so that she can at least think about how much You want to love her and take care of her.

MY PRAYER NOW:

Thank You for this afternoon. Thank You for helping me feel better. I had a great time sewing on buttons with Gabby. I think I've probably wrecked my clothes but hey-de-ho.

THURSDAY 18 FEBRUARY

Still raining. Gabby opened the curtains and everything was grey and drippy.

'Do you fancy doing some painting?' she said.

'What kind of painting?' I asked.

'Oh, you know,' she said, 'I thought we could paint my bedroom bright purple with big green spots on the ceiling. If we're really quick, no one'll find out until it's too late.'

'What?' I said.

'Joke,' she said.

'Right,' I said. (Gabby didn't seem like the sort of person to make a joke.)

'What kind of painting do you think?' she said.

'OK,' I said, 'I'd love to paint.'

So we painted. All morning.

I painted a picture of Uncle Rich's and Auntie Chrissie's house. Then I painted Gabby's tree house. Then I had a go at painting a cow in the field at the bottom of the garden. You wouldn't really know it was a cow though. It was quite fat and splodgy. In fact most of my painting was quite fat and splodgy. Mind you, I had a fat splodge of a paintbrush so I suppose it wasn't really surprising. Gabby had the thin one. I showed her my cow.

I said, 'What do you think it is?'

She said, 'Mmm – a cushion?'

I know. Tragic.

Gabby's painting wasn't a bit like mine. She didn't paint things. Not houses or animals or people. Everything was patterns, swirls and blobs and zigzaggy lines.

And she always
chose dark colours,
purple and black and a sort of sludge she
made by mixing purple and green.

I said, 'Do you always do patterns?'

'Yup.'

I said, 'Is that so you don't end up
painting a cow that looks like a cushion?'

'Nope. I could probably paint a cow that
looks like a cow.'

'Go on, then,' I said. 'Prove it.'

Gabby just said, 'I don't have to prove
anything. I just paint what I like to paint.
We had this lady who came to the children's
home. She was an art therapist, or something.
She tried to get us to paint our feelings. She said
however we were feeling, no matter if it was sad, angry,
happy, zany – well, she didn't exactly say zany, but that
can be a feeling too, can't it, so that's why I said it
– anyway, no matter what our feelings were, it was
good to be able to put them down on paper. It would
help us to understand what was going on inside us.'

'And did it help?' I asked.

'Of course not,' she said 'Well, not then anyway. I just
thought, "What a load of rubbish!", and instead I made
everyone cross by scooping loads of paint onto my
paintbrush, then flicking it all round the room.'

'Mrs Parker would hit the roof at least several
times if I did anything like that at school,' I said. I was a
bit shocked actually. 'Didn't you get into trouble?'

'Oh, yeah,' she said, as if getting into trouble was one

of those normal things she did all the time. 'I wasn't allowed to go to painting sessions anymore. I didn't care though. I was glad. Rose said they'd had someone like this art therapy person at another children's home where she'd stayed. She said that sooner or later we'd be told to start painting things that made us feel happy – like a garden or the seaside or trees (although why trees should make you feel happy I really haven't a clue). Then we'd have to move on to painting people we might remember who'd been kind to us. I mean, there was no way I was <u>ever</u> going to do that.'

'Why not?' I asked. I wondered if Gabby couldn't remember anyone ever being kind to her.

'Because I just wasn't,' she said. 'It's all private, stuff like that. It's got nothing to do with anyone else.'

Gabby was twizzling her paintbrush round and round in the purple paint. I was thinking, I hope she doesn't start flicking it. I'm wearing my favourite top.

'So, that's why you only paint patterns?' I said carefully. If Gabby thought I was being nosey, it could be bye-bye lovely yellow T-shirt with little white dots and hello messy slop top with dollopy purple splots.

'Well,' Gabby said, beginning to put dollopy purple splodges on her paper (phew), 'I started thinking one day that maybe the art therapist person was right about painting your feelings. Maybe it could be helpful. I thought it might be sort of like talking about them without having to <u>actually</u> talk about them. If you see what I mean.'

Not really, no. Sarah and me, we're always talking about how we feel. We love it. Painting purple splodges just wouldn't be the same at all.

'So anyway,' Gabby said, 'I decided to give it a try. And I liked it. The best thing is that no one else knows what I'm painting because all they can see is blobs and squiggles. But I know.'

There was a really interesting squiggle on the top right hand corner of her paper. I was dying to ask what it was. Too risky, though. Better never to know than to get splatter-painted purple.

TODAY'S PRAYER FOR GABBY:

Dear God, I can't imagine not wanting to talk about feelings. Sarah and I do it all the time. Sometimes she can help me and sometimes I can help her. In fact I'd say that the Topz Gang know just about all of each others' feelings just about all of the time, because we don't hide anything from each other. Why would you hide things from your friends? If you're sad you'd want them to know so they could cheer you up and if you're happy you'd want them to know so they could be happy with you. I don't think Gabby's ever really had anyone to be happy or sad with. I think she just keeps all her feelings to herself because she doesn't trust anyone enough to ask them to listen to her. Maybe she thinks she'll be laughed at. Or worse, maybe she thinks no one will care anyway. Or maybe she just feels that no one will understand, so what's the point in saying anything.

Lord God, if only she knew You, she'd know that she could tell You anything. She'd know that You'd listen to her going on about whatever she wanted to go on about whenever she wanted to go on about it. She'd know she could talk to You in the night instead of just lying there crying. And she'd realise there's no need to hide her feelings away in paintings because You know what they are anyway.

Help Gabby to find You, Lord. Help me to be brave enough to tell her who You are. And help her to see that all I want is to be her friend. Just like You do. Amen.

After lunch

STILL raining. Mum rang. She says it's not raining at home. Typical. She also said that when she came out of the supermarket earlier, Benny almost ran into her on his skateboard. Also typical.

Groovy-doovy, though, she's redecorating my bedroom. She said it was going to be a surprise only she's not very good at keeping secrets.

I said to Gabby, 'Mum's redecorating my bedroom.'

Gabby said, 'Oh, how lovely for you,' as if she didn't think it was lovely at all, and went upstairs. She'd gone all moody.

My fault. I shouldn't mention home. I shouldn't say anything about it. It sets her off. She's jealous, I suppose. I would be, too. If someone went on to me about her family and I didn't have one, I'd hate it, I know I would. I used to get jealous when some of my friends started to get mobile phones and Dad said I couldn't have one till I went to secondary school. And that was just about a stupid old phone! Imagine how you'd feel if practically everyone around you had a family and you didn't and all you wanted in the whole world was your own mum and dad.

Caley says I've just got to be me. But how can I be me when I can't talk about home? I suppose I just mustn't, though. Talking about something Gabby'll never have (at least not in the way she wants) seems really unkind. What I've got to do is find a way to talk about God. I mean, I can't give Gabby a home or a family, but I can tell her about Someone who wants to be her Father in heaven. I can tell her He's there waiting for her. I SO wish Sarah was here. Then we could tell her together.

Supper time

Got to be quick – Auntie Chrissie's just putting supper out. Apparently she's <u>made</u> ice cream for pudding. She's got a special thingy for doing it in. And her ice cream's got real strawberries in it! Auntie Chrissie grew loads last summer in the garden and she still had some in the freezer.

I said to Gabby, 'You've got to admit it is pretty brilliant – I mean, living with a family that not only has homemade honey and homemade bread, but homemade ice cream with homemade strawberries in it as well!'

Gabby didn't say anything but I'm absolutely positive she was trying not to smile.

Anyway, anyway, anyway – just had the **most** **wickedly wicked afternoon!**

Josh and Caley took us tenpin bowling. In the village where they live, there's not much in the way of bowling alleys and stuff, but there's this little town about twenty minutes' drive away and that's where we all went. Josh drove the car!

I said, 'Wow, Josh! I didn't realise you were as old as that!'

Caley said, 'I know. It's hard to believe he's 105, isn't it?'

Bowling has put Gabby in SUCH a good mood. I'm not surprised either. She's fantastic at it. Loads better than Caley and me and easily as good as Josh – and he's absolutely brilliant (which you have to admit is quite incredible for someone who's 105 years old).

Supper's on the table. Got to go. We've got lasagne for first course, which is my total favourite. Big problem, though: how am I going to make myself NOT eat too much lasagne so that I've got plenty of room left for homemade strawberry ice cream? Tricky …

Bedtime
My tummy is still SO full. Benny and Paul would go absolutely crazy here.

FRIDAY 19 FEBRUARY

It should have been all right. After yesterday everything should have been all right.

But she's been through the top drawer. Gabby's been through the top drawer of the big chest under the window. That's where Auntie Chrissie said I could keep some of my stuff. I've got clean T-shirts in there, a towel and a book Sarah lent me. And my diary. Underneath everything else, that's where I've been keeping my diary.

After breakfast Gabby disappeared upstairs. She wasn't in the bathroom when I went to look for her, so I knew she must be in the bedroom. I thought, I'll sneak up on her and say, 'Boo!' like Sarah does to me sometimes in the cloakroom at school. I opened the door really quietly. Gabby never heard a thing.

And there she was. The top drawer of the chest was open. One of my T-shirts was on the floor. Gabby was standing by the window with my diary in her hands.

I just stared. I couldn't believe it. I know she made comments about all the writing I did but I never thought she'd want to know that badly what I'd been saying. I mean, how could she? How could she read my private diary like that? She was always going on about keeping her private stuff private. Didn't she think I might have stuff I wanted to keep private too?

All those things I'd written about her. They weren't nasty things (apart from the Gobby Gabby bit which I should never have even thought let alone written down), they were just things that came into my head, things I felt. But I never in a million years would want her to see them. She'd hate me. She'd hate me forever.

'Gabby! That's my diary!' I said.

She didn't answer. She just looked at me.

'You can't read that,' I said.

'It's mine. It's my private stuff. I'd never read your private stuff.'

Gabby still didn't say anything.

'Give it back,' I said.

'Give it back now.'

Auntie Chrissie must have heard me. She was up the stairs in no time.

'What's going on?' she said.

'Nothing!' Gabby snapped. 'Nothing's going on. Josie seems to think I've been reading her stupid diary, that's all. Well I haven't. As if I'd be interested in the boring old rubbish she's been writing anyway.'

'But you're looking at it,' I said. 'You've been in the drawer and taken it out and you're looking at it.'

'No I'm not!' she shouted, 'I'm not interested in your pathetic, sad little diary. OK?'

I had to dodge then because she threw it at me.

'Gabby!' shouted Auntie Chrissie. Auntie Chrissie never shouts. Well, I've never heard her shout. I don't think Gabby had ever heard her shout either. Next thing, she pushed right past us. She actually shoved Auntie Chrissie out of the way.

Caley says she saw her run out to the tree house. It's pouring with rain. She hasn't got her coat on or anything. Auntie Chrissie says we've got to leave her on her own for a while. She says sometimes children like Gabby need some space. A bit of time out. That's why Uncle Rich built the tree house.

I can't believe it, though. I don't know what I'm going to do. Supposing she did read the bit where I wrote Gobby Gabby. Supposing she read where I said all I wanted was to go home. Supposing she read my prayers.

After lunch

Gabby still hasn't come back inside. Auntie Chrissie's been out three times to see if she's all right. Last time she went she took Gabby's coat. She says the tree house roof's got bit of a leak. It's only small but drops of rain are dripping through it and apparently the wind's whooshing in at the door opening and the window. She thinks Gabby's going to catch cold. Gabby won't come in, though. Whatever Auntie Chrissie says, she just refuses. And I bet she won't put her coat on either.

Later

Auntie Chrissie says I shouldn't go out. She says we should all leave Gabby alone until she feels ready to come back in the house.

But what if she doesn't? What if she decides she's never going to leave the tree house ever again?

Unless she's just waiting. Maybe she's thinking to herself, I'll only go back in the house when that horrible Josie goes home. That could be it, you know. After all, Mum and Dad are coming for me in the morning. She might decide she'd be all right up there in the tree for just one cold, drippy night.

And what happens if I see Sarah tomorrow? She'll want to know everything that's happened – how great it all was, how exciting, how fantasmagorical (Sarah language).

And all I'll be able to say is, 'Yeah, it was cool. Gabby and I didn't know what to say to each other first of all. Most of the time she didn't even seem to like me. Then, guess what? Just when we were starting to get on, this really major thing happened and, as far as I know, she's still sitting in a leaky old tree house and is never going to have anything to do with anyone on the planet ever again. Especially not me.'

I mean, how fantasmagorical is that?

Later later

It's raining even harder. It looks as if someone's shooting water up at the window out of a hosepipe. Auntie Chrissie keeps saying she's so sorry about everything. She says maybe it was too soon to ask me to come and stay and perhaps she should have given Gabby more time to settle in with them first. She even asked if I wanted Uncle Rich to take me home when he got back later. I said I'd think about it.

I've thought about it, though and, no, I can't go home. Not until everything's sorted out. Gabby may not like me that much and she'll probably never want me to be her friend now (not that she did in the first place), but what would God think if I just left without ever speaking to her again? Anyway, I need to go and say sorry in case she read the Gobby Gabby bit in my diary. She might not have got as far as the part where I wrote I'm sorry.

Auntie Chrissie said I shouldn't go out and see her but I've got to. I've got to see her and that's it.

Later later later!

GABBY'S COME IN!

Finally, she's come in out of the tree house. She's having a hot bath. She was all shivery and cold and damp, so Auntie Chrissie thought that would be the best way to warm up. I'm cold and damp too but not nearly as much as Gabby. I did go out, you see. I suddenly had this brainwave. I thought, what do Sarah and I do when we have a fall out? I mean, to be honest, we SO hardly ever have fall outs and they're SO not serious, but if we do have one, the thing we always do is TALK. It's different because Sarah's my best friend and we know each other mega incredibly well, so talking's just easy peasy lemon squeezy. But, on the other hand, I thought, Gabby's been huddled up in a drippy tree house for hours and hours and hours and maybe the reason she's not coming back indoors is because she thinks I don't want to see her as much as she doesn't want to see me. And that is SO not true.

I was right about Gabby not putting her coat on. When I stuck my head through the tree house door, I could see it just lying in a heap beside her on the floor.

I said, 'Aren't you freezing?'

Gabby said, 'What do you care?' (She didn't seem the slightest bit surprised to see me – which I actually found slightly surprising.)

I said, 'I do care, if you really want to know. I don't want you to catch your freezing absolute death of cold just because of me.'

Gabby said, 'I'm not catching my freezing absolute death of anything.'

'Right,' I said.

Then everything else I wanted to say all sort of came tumbling out in a big splurge. I opened my mouth and –

'Anyway, I'm going home tomorrow and I just wanted you to know that I really don't care that you read my diary. It's stupid anyway. I just write whatever comes into my head. And I'm really sorry if you read the bit where I called you Gobby Gabby. It's just I was so upset that you dropped Sarah's character profile on the floor. I mean, she worked really hard on it for you. And she'd be such a good friend to you even though you're obviously not interested in having friends, which actually I think is just silly if there are people around who <u>want</u> to be your friends. Like me, for instance. And Sarah, for another instance. So I'm sorry, all right, and I'm sorry if you read anything else in there that annoyed you, like my prayers and stuff. But, like I said, it's just what's in my head. And I had to talk to God about you because He loves you so much and wants you to be His friend. I mean, I had to ask Him to help you find Him, didn't I? Only it all seems to have gone wrong now and it's probably my fault … So anyway, staying out here all night is just, well, SO not a good thing to do. And … will you please come back into the house now? We don't have to sit in the same room. I can go and lock myself in the toilet if it'll make you feel more comfortable.'

Silence. Nothing. Gabby said nothing at all.

I crouched down on the floor. I'd made up my mind I wasn't leaving until we'd sorted things out. Unfortunately I'd crouched right under the leak in the roof. A drop of rain slipped down my neck and wriggled its way wetly down my back. Eeeew.

Then it happened. One of those 'opposite' moments – ie one of those moments when you think you know

EXACTLY what's going to happen next, only to find that when the next thing actually happens, it turns out to be the complete opposite. In fact, I couldn't have got it more wrong.

Gabby sat staring at me. Her eyes were fixed on my face. She looked as if she just could <u>not</u> believe I was capable of so much wittering. (I don't think about it, you see. I just open my mouth and all this stuff pours out. Sarah's used to the way I witter. She says I've got 'witterability' which, sometimes, can be quite impressive.)

Then, all of a sudden, Gabby started to laugh. She didn't shout at me, or call me names, or say she wished she'd never met me like I thought she probably would, she laughed. And laughed and laughed.

I wasn't sure what to do. I didn't feel like laughing myself so I thought perhaps I should just wait until she stopped. Which she did do – eventually. (Unlike the rain which was still coming down by the bucketful and trickling more and more through the roof, then down my neck like a mini waterfall. It felt as though I had something like a small pond collecting in the waistband of my jeans.)

'Did you really call me Gobby Gabby?'

That's what Gabby said. When she finally stopped laughing.

I think my mouth may have dropped open at this point. Gabby obviously hadn't seen that bit. Whatever else she may have read in my diary, she hadn't seen that I'd called her Gobby Gabby. And now I'd just told her.

'Well …' I began. 'I didn't exactly mean … You see, what I was thinking … It was only because of … What I'm trying to say is …'

'Don't worry about it,' Gabby said (which was just as well because I couldn't seem to remember how to finish a sentence). 'I think it's funny. Not if anyone else had said it maybe, but it's funny that you said it. I never thought someone like you would ever call anyone a name.'

'What do you mean, someone like me?' I said.

'I don't know. You just seem so … nice.'

'What, nice in a good way?' I said.

Gabby shrugged. 'Nicer than me, anyway. And I wasn't reading your diary. Whatever you think, I really wasn't.'

'But you got it out of the drawer,' I said. 'Why did you do that if you weren't going to read it?'

She didn't answer for a moment. Then, very slowly, she pulled something out of the pocket of her jeans. It was paper, all folded up and a bit soggy-looking. She held it out to me. I took it, but I didn't need to open it to know what it was. All of a sudden I realised. All of a sudden I understood what Gabby had been after. How could I have been so stupid? I'd written loads in my diary since I'd found her with it. I couldn't believe I hadn't noticed: there was nothing slipped inside the back cover. The two character profiles weren't there where I'd put them. Gabby had taken them.

She sniffed and rubbed her nose with the back of her hand. I didn't know if she was going to cry.

'I just wanted to have another look,' she said. 'I thought, you seem to be an OK sort of person so maybe Sarah's an OK sort of person too. Then, when I opened your diary, I found the other profile with Sarah's. The one for God. So I thought I may as well read that one as well.'

'Why didn't you say?' I asked. 'Why didn't you just tell me?'

'Dunno,' she shrugged. 'I was angry, I suppose. You just assumed I was doing something wrong.'

She sniffed again, then –

'Anyway, shall we go back in the house now?' she said. 'I don't know about you but I'm absolutely freezing.'

In bed

We did it! We talked! Gabby and me,

we talked properly. Almost as soon as she'd had her bath, she started asking me questions – about Sarah, about home, about Topz – and about GOD! It was unbelievable! I mean, if I hadn't heard it all for myself, I'd never have believed it. I told Gabby how much God loves her and how He'll never let her down. I told her that she doesn't ever need to feel lonely because He'll always be there to listen to her and be close to her. I don't know if what I said made much sense, but at least I got to say it.

Gabby must have thought a lot about it, too, because after supper she said, 'I used to think about God. I used to think about Him lots after … my mum got ill. And I can see why someone like God would love you and Sarah. Like I say, you're OK people. But why would He love me? I'm not an OK person. I'm not nice like you are. I haven't got my own family. I don't even know where my dad's gone. The only reason I'm living here is because I've been put here, not because anyone really wants me here. Why would God love someone nobody wants?'

What could I say? It was so sad. I could tell Gabby that Uncle Rich and Auntie Chrissie really did want her here but I couldn't make her feel any different. No wonder Gabby didn't want me as a friend. How can you make friends if you think you're no good and nobody wants you? If you don't like yourself, how can you believe anyone else is going to like you? I couldn't let her see what I was thinking, though. She'd hate it if she thought I was feeling sorry for her. She'd think that's the only reason I was being kind.

'You see,' I said (hoping, hoping, HOPING she'd understand), 'it's because you feel all on your own and unwanted that God wants to love you even more. It's up to you to trust Him, though. And that means you've got to let Him in.'

I don't know whether Gabby will let God in. I'm not really sure whether she's let me in or whether this is just a one-off chatty moment that'll never happen again. But when I gave her back the character profiles and said she could keep them because, after all, she's the one Sarah and I had written them for, she didn't drop them on the floor. She didn't smile or anything, either, or say thank you, she just nodded.

But a moment later, when she thought I wasn't looking, out of the corner of my eye I saw her unfold them, smooth them out and slip them under her pillow.

SATURDAY 20 FEBRUARY

Just packed up all my stuff. Mum and Dad'll be here in about an hour. I can't believe I'm going home already. Not that I don't want to go home because I really do. It's just, well, almost a whole week can seem to be going incredibly slowly and then suddenly it's all over and you realise that actually almost a whole week is like nothing. Gone in a flash. Whiz-bang-crash.

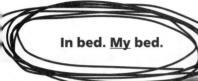

In bed. <u>My</u> bed.

Hello, bed. Here I am
again. Actually I nearly wasn't.
When I rang Sarah to say I was home,
she was so excited she wanted me to go straight
round to her house and sleep over and everything.
Only Mum and Dad said it would be quite nice to have
me home tonight because I'd been away all week
(almost). I'm glad really. I mean, sleeping over at
Sarah's would be cool, just maybe not tonight. Tonight
I want to be at home.

My bedroom looks wicked. I wish Gabby could see
it. Mum's done it in blue. I've got new curtains, too,
with big swirls all over them. They remind me of one of
Gabby's 'feelings' paintings.

It was weird when we said goodbye to each other.
All awkward and uncomfortable like when we said
hello last weekend. You'd never think we'd just been
together for almost a week. You'd never think we'd had
any special chats. In fact, you'd never think we knew
each other at all. Gabby didn't even come out to the car,
she just stayed in the kitchen.

I said, 'I'll write to you. I'll send you loads of letters all the time so you don't forget me.' I thought that might make her laugh. It didn't.

I said, 'I had a really great time.'

I hoped she might say, yes, so did she. She didn't.

'And I really, really like you,' I said when everyone else had gone outside ready to wave us off.

'And I'm always going to think of you as <u>my</u> friend even if you don't want to think of me as <u>yours</u>.'

I waited hopefully.

Gabby said, 'You'd better go.

I think your mum and dad are ready.'

And that was that.

Not much of a goodbye.

Not a goodbye at all.

PRAYER FOR GABBY:
Lord, please be with Gabby forever and ever. Amen.

SUNDAY 21 FEBRUARY

Back to school tomorrow. Drama Club will be starting
this week. Exciting or what? At least, I was excited
about it before I went away. Now it doesn't seem that
important. Dad says I look sad. I'm not sad, though. I
don't really know what I am. But definitely not sad.

After church

Wow, that was weird. When I walked into church
this morning it was a bit like being a famous person
off the telly. The minute I was inside the door, I
was surrounded, honestly, totally and completely
surrounded, by every single one of the Topz Gang and
some of the others from Sunday Club as well. Even
Louise bounded over (and, believe me, Louise may
be quite energetic, but she doesn't often bound) and
wanted to know if I'd had a cool time away and how
I'd got on with Gabby. In fact it was Gabby everyone
wanted to know about. I think she must be the one
who's famous, not me. No point telling her, though.
She'd never believe me.

Evening

Talk about talking the hind legs off a donkey, or
whatever that saying is! I think Sarah and I must have
talked the hind legs off about four donkeys, and their
front legs <u>and</u> their tails as well! I know what it is. You
see, all half term I've done about one million trillionth
of the talking I usually do. Sarah's done even less than
that, because she tends to have even more to say to me
than I have to say to her. So this afternoon after lunch
when she came over, we just had SO much to say and
SO much to yabber on about. It all came out in a sort

of gushing river of words mixed up with rolling around on the floor laughing (I've SO missed rolling around on the floor laughing), and it went on for hours. Dad says, with all the energy we were putting into talking we could probably have produced enough electricity to power the whole of London for at least three months.

Personally, I think he's just jealous because he probably couldn't talk for long enough to power a pocket torch for five minutes.

There were a few awkward bits – like when Sarah asked me if Gabby had liked her character profile. I didn't want to tell her the bad stuff.

I said, 'She seemed to want to keep it in the end, so I think she must have liked it. She's just quite worried about having friends. She thinks everyone's going to end up leaving her on her own so it's best to stay on your own in the first place.'

Sarah said, 'What, on your own and friendless? Why would anyone want that? Anyway, we're not going to leave her on her own. Didn't you tell her that?'

'Of course I did,' I said. 'And it was brilliant because, even though I didn't actually get round to showing it to her, she sort of accidentally found the profile we did of God, which meant I could tell her even more about Him. It's just …'

'What?'

'It's just it must be so hard to understand that God

wants to know you and to love you if you don't even believe that there are any ordinary <u>people</u> who want to know you and love you.'

'Are you going to write to her?' Sarah asked.

'I told her I'd write her letters,' I said.

'And what did she say? Did she say she'd write back?'

'She didn't really say anything,' I said. 'She probably thought I'd get home and forget all about her and not bother. She doesn't think anyone wants to bother.'

'Mmm,' said Sarah meaningfully. 'Then I think we should bother right now.'

So that's what we did. We bothered and we wrote Gabby a letter.

Dear Gabby,

I'm writing this letter to you with Sarah. So you know which one of us wrote which bits, this first part is written by me and this is my hand writing, and Sarah's going to write her bits in capital letters. Hope you don't get confused. Hope we don't get confused either.

Has it stopped raining, yet? If not, is the tree house flooded? Come to that, is your ordinary house flooded? I don't think I've ever seen as much rain as you seem to get in the country. Apparently it's hardly rained at all here. I'm sure I must have shrunk at least four centimetres while I was staying with you. Not that I care, though. All the same, it might be an idea if you measure yourself on a regular basis, just to make sure all the wetness isn't shrinking you down into a mini-sized version of yourself.

Oops, I think I'm starting to witter, so I'll pass you over to Sarah.

HI GABBY. THIS IS SARAH. YOU'LL KNOW IT'S ME BECAUSE OF MY FUNKY CAPITAL LETTER WRITING. I'VE JUST THOUGHT, IF JOSIE IS WITTERING ON, I SUPPOSE THAT MUST MEAN SHE'S A WITTERER. IN WHICH CASE, I WONDER IF THAT MAKES YOU A WITTEREE – I.E. SOMEONE WHO IS ON THE RECEIVING END OF HER WITTERINGS?

Hello, me again. The reason Sarah is such an expert on wittering is because she does so much of it herself.

ANYWAY, HOW DID YOU MANAGE TO SURVIVE BEING WITH JOSIE IN THE RAIN FOR A WHOLE WEEK?

It was only almost a whole week actually.

THAT'S THE TROUBLE WITH WITTERERS. THEY CAN BE SO PICKY. OW. (IF MY WRITING'S A BIT SCRIBBLY-SCRAWLY FROM NOW ON, IT'S NOT MY FAULT. JOSIE JUST WAPPED ME ON THE HEAD WITH HER PILLOW.)

Some people's heads are just perfect for wapping with pillows, don't you think, Gabby?

I KNOW YOU LIVE QUITE A LONG WAY AWAY, BUT IF YOU EVER WANT TO COME AND STAY HERE AND MEET ALL OF US AND JOIN IN ALL THE WACKY STUFF WE DO, YOU'D BE SO TRIPLE AMAZINGLY WELCOME. NONE OF THE TOPZ GANG HAS A TREE HOUSE (YOURS, BY THE WAY, SOUNDS JUST FANTASMAGORICALLY WICKED), BUT DANNY'S REALLY CLEVER AND INTO MAKING DENS JUST ABOUT ANYWHERE. HE BUILT A FANTASTIC ONE BEHIND THE CHANGING HUTS AT SCHOOL OUT OF PLASTIC BOXES AND A BIT OF OLD CARPET HE FOUND IN THE PE SHED. UNFORTUNATELY MR MALLORY (TEACHER) DISCOVERED IT AND SAID HE HAD TO TAKE IT DOWN BECAUSE IT LOOKED UNTIDY. UNTIDY! AS IF ANYONE EVER GOES BEHIND THE CHANGING HUTS ANYWAY (OTHER THAN PEOPLE WHO WANT TO BUILD DENS, THAT IS).

BY THE WAY, DID I MENTION THAT IT WOULD BE ACEY-GRACEY IF YOU CAME TO STAY? I REALLY MEAN THAT. I'M

AFRAID YOU WOULD HAVE TO MEET MY TWIN BROTHER, JOHN, BUT I SUPPOSE NOTHING'S PERFECT.

There's only one bed in my room but we've got a fold-up bed, too. Sarah sleeps on it when she stays over. It's ever so comfy. In fact, sometimes when she stays, we swap and she sleeps in my bed so that I can have a go on the fold-up one. If you do decide to come and visit, you can choose whichever bed you'd like.

Do you know what, I think we're all wittered out for now, so thanks SO much for having me to stay and we'll write again soon.

VERY SOON. IF YOU WANT TO WRITE BACK IN THE MEANTIME THAT WOULD BE SUPERLY DUPERLY. SEE YOU VERY SOON.

Yes. See you.

Lots and lots of love Josie **AND SARAH** XXXXXX

Sarah said, 'Gabby'll <u>definitely</u> come and visit now. When do you think she'll write back?'

'Soon, I hope,' I said.

'Soon, I hope, too,' Sarah said.

I want her to write back straightaway. I know that's what I'd do if I got a letter like that. Gabby's different from me, though, and different from Sarah. Everything's more complicated with her. Part of me isn't sure she'll write back at all but I wasn't going to tell Sarah that.

'By the way,' Sarah said cheerfully, 'you never told me what Gabby's short for.'

'That's because I don't know,' I said.

'You don't know?' said Sarah frowning. 'Didn't you ask?'

'No,' I said.

'Why not?' Sarah said. 'I would have asked.'

I don't think you would, actually, I thought. If it had been you staying with Gabby and trying to show her you were her friend, I really don't think you would have asked anything. With Gabby, it's as if everything's a secret. It's all wrapped up tight and hidden away. She doesn't want anyone to know anything. And if someone doesn't want you to know, you can't really ask.

Bedtime

I said to Mum, 'Do you think I could ring Sarah?'

She said, 'Whatever for? Didn't you do enough talking this afternoon?'

'Not quite,' I said.

'Is this about Gabby?'

'Probably.'

'Thought it might be.'

'So can I?'

'Go on, then. But, please, be quick.'

I was quick.

I said to Sarah, 'I've been thinking. About our letter. There's something I want to add.'

'What?'

'I want to tell Gabby how amazing she is because God

74

made her. He planned her. He knew her even before she was born.'

'So tell her, then,' said Sarah.

'Do you think I should?' I said.

'Definitely,' said Sarah.

'You don't think it's being too pushy?' I said.

'How can you be too pushy about telling someone they're amazing,' Sarah said.

Good point.

you're amazing

I got out the letter and wrote:

P.S. Just to let you know that you're amazing, Gabby. It says so in the Bible. It says God planned you and made you. He knows everything about you. He knew you before you were even born. That's what He's like, you see – He loves you to total pieces and has always loved you, right from your very, very beginning, no matter what else has happened. Please talk to Him about your sad stuff. Just give it to Him. All He wants is to take it away and show you how to like yourself and be happy.

Lots and lots of love again J

I can't change it now. I've got to leave it. I put it straight in the envelope and sealed it up. Then Mum got a stamp from one of the pockets in her purse and stuck it on. Gabby's letter's by the telephone on the hall table ready to put in the post box tomorrow morning.

MONDAY 22 FEBRUARY

Sarah said, 'Did you post it?'

I said, 'Yes.'

Sarah said, 'Did you add the extra bit about Gabby being amazing?'

I said, 'Yes.'

Sarah said, 'Cool bananas. We might even get a letter back before the weekend, mightn't we?'

I said, 'Yes.'

That's what I said.

But who knows?

TUESDAY 23 FEBRUARY

'Gabby ought to get our letter today.'

That's the first thing Sarah said to me this morning.

'Yes,' I said.

Sarah said, 'She might even have read it already.'

'Yes,' I said.

Sarah said, 'Wouldn't it be so snazzy if she wrote back right away and then we got her letter tomorrow?'

'Yes,' I said.

I'm in a yessy mood.

After supper

Have you noticed how sometimes school is just blah, blah, blah, yawn, yawn and more blah? Especially when you've just come back after something like half term and all you really feel like doing is racing about kicking a football or doing cool stuff in tree houses or dens or anywhere, in fact, just as long as it isn't school. That's what I thought the next few weeks were going to be – all words and numbers and even MORE stuff to do with wrinkly old kings and queens from about a hundred million years ago. Actually, though, it's quite creepily weird how totally wrong you can be sometimes ('you' meaning me, obviously).

It was like that after morning break.

Paul said, 'Do you think Mrs Parker is doing some sort of special brain stretching exercises or something? I mean, first she came up with the drama club idea, and now this.'

And 'this' is absolutely whiz-the-dizz!

Mrs Parker marched into the classroom and said (without waiting for us to be quiet or anything like she usually does), 'Right. I want you all to look down and then close your eyes.'

We didn't. We all looked at each other. Well, you would, wouldn't you? I mean, the last thing teachers normally ask you to do is close your eyes. Normally it's all, 'Watch what you're doing,' and, 'Look at the board,' and 'Haven't you got eyes in your head?'

Mrs Parker clapped her hands. 'Come on. I want to see everyone's heads down and eyes shut.'

So we did it. We all put our heads down and shut our eyes. (I suppose we all did anyway. I couldn't see. I had my eyes shut. Tee hee.)

Whatever was coming next, though, it had to be so much more interesting than that mini beast project I thought we'd be finishing today. Not that I've got anything against mini beasts. Some of them are actually quite cute in their own many-legged way. I'm just not in the mood for drawing woodlice.

'Now,' Mrs Parker went on, 'I'm going to hold up a picture and I want you to tell me what it's a picture of. But don't open your eyes. You must keep them closed.'

Silence. More than just silence. Stunned silence.

'Can't anyone tell me what this is a picture of?' asked Mrs Parker. 'All right, let's try another one. What's this?'

I was dying to look at Sarah. I was honestly beginning to think Mrs Parker had lost her marbles – which is pretty bad news for a teacher when you think about it.

Then, all of a sudden, someone laughed. Well, it wasn't exactly a laugh. It was more of a splurt. I think it was Charlotte Miller. It sounded like that annoying, snorty kind of thing she does. And then, of course, everyone started to laugh.

Whoops, I thought, now Mrs Parky's going to throw a spectacular wobbly.

She didn't, though. She started laughing too.

HA HA HA.

'All right, everyone, open your eyes,' she said (not that anyone still had their eyes shut by that time). 'So, who spotted the deliberate mistake?' (You know, how can you see a picture with your eyes closed?)

Anyway, turns out this was all about being blind. Mrs Parker started talking about how much you miss if you're a blind person and how important it is for people who can see to find ways of helping blind people to see, too. She said that blind people 'see' with their hands and fingers. They feel the shapes of different things and that gives them an idea of what those things must look like.

'But,' she said, 'supposing a blind person wants to enjoy a picture of some kind – a photo or a painting. How can they? They can't see it and there's nothing to feel because it's just a flat surface. So, what we're going to do is create a picture that blind people can see.'

Blind children, actually. We're going to be making this huge collage. We've got to use as many different touchy-feely materials as we can think of and collect, like feathers, scrunched up tissue paper, furry cloth, cotton wool, seashells, even pasta. Then we've got to set them all out to make this fantastic picture. And you'll never guess what it's going to be a picture of – Noah's Ark!

When it's done (and this is the best bit), it's going to be put up in the blind school that's near here for all the children there! Mrs Parker says they'll be able to 'see' Noah's Ark because they'll be able to feel it. She even said perhaps we could include a recording of different animal noises as part of the display so that the blind children could use their sense of hearing to help them see as well as their sense of touch. I mean, triple wowzy or what! To be honest I'm not normally an arty sort of person. I'd never have got this excited about drawing woodlice – which, by the way, I'm not going to have to do now for at least three weeks because that's how long we're going to be working on this collage.

When I told Benny, he said, 'Don't you ever have to do any work in your class?'

Paul said, 'Of course we do. Just not as much as you because we're just SO much more clever.'

Bedtime

Sarah rang.

She said, 'If a letter from Gabby comes tomorrow morning, you will bring it into school, won't you?'

'Of course I will, but the post doesn't normally get here till after I've gone for the bus,' I said. 'Actually, Sarah, I've been thinking.'

I <u>had</u> been thinking, too. A lot. Even Dad noticed.

He said, 'What's going on? How come you're so quiet?'

I said, 'I'm thinking.'

He said, 'They must be very deep thoughts.'

I said, 'They are.'

And they REALLY are, too. Because what I've been thinking about is Gabby. It's all to do with this blind picture.

So I said to Sarah, 'You know this picture we're doing for the blind school? Well, all I keep thinking about is Gabby – which is dead odd because you'd think I'd be thinking about the blind children, wouldn't you? Anyway, I suddenly realised what it is.'

'And what is it?' said Sarah.

I said, 'Well, Gabby's like one of the blind children, isn't she? The blind children can't see what's around them, so they need help. They need other people to find different ways of showing them how to see because their eyes don't work. Well, Gabby can't <u>see</u> God. So many people have let her down and she feels so lonely that I don't think she can really understand what love is. And unless she can start understanding what it's like to be loved by people, how will she <u>ever</u> be able to see Him? How will she ever be able to let Him be her loving Father? I mean, God is love, isn't He? That's what the Bible says. But Gabby, she can't even see <u>herself</u> properly. After everything that's happened to her, all she can see inside herself is this person that she thinks no one wants and isn't good enough. Don't you see what that means?'

'No,' said Sarah.

'It means, it's up to us to help her to "see" God. Just like we're going to find ways of showing Noah's Ark to the blind children by making a picture of it for them that they can touch and feel, that's what we've got to do for Gabby. We've got to find ways of showing God's love to her that she can understand.'

'Mmm, that's really clever,' said Sarah. 'Only … how are we going to do that, then?'

'Dunno,' I said. 'I'm thinking.'

In bed

It's not just Gabby, is it? There must be 'blind' people all over the world – people who, for one reason or another, can't 'see' God.

Dad just came in.

'Still thinking?' he asked.

'Yup,' I said.

'You've probably got a thinker's brain,' he said.

'Yup,' I said.

'I expect you get that from me,' he said.

I didn't say anything.

WEDNESDAY 24 FEBRUARY

That's it. I want to be an actor! So does Sarah. And Benny. And Paul. In fact all of us in Topz want to be actors. Even Danny, and usually all he wants to be is sporty. Drama club was so brilliant! Mrs Parker is just … BRILLIANT! What more can I say?

We started off with some hilarious drama games. 'Warm-ups' Mrs Parker called them, but actually they were more like 'get into daft mode-ups'. Benny had to be a football. Yes, that's right, a football. With a blindfold on. We played this game of footie with him where we had to sort of 'pass' him to each other – in slow motion! We weren't actually allowed to kick him obviously, we had to pretend to do the kicking bit ('very slowly and with total control,' Mrs Parker said), and Benny knew it was time to move when the kicker touched him on the shoulder. Mrs Parker said this was a trust exercise. Because Benny was wearing the blindfold and couldn't see where he was going, he had to trust that all the kickers would look after him and send him off in the right direction, then 'catch' him again so that he wouldn't bump into anything.

Of course, being Benny, he really got into actually <u>being</u> the football. He did all this rolling and spinning and bouncing.

'And, believe me,' he said afterwards, 'it's not easy to bounce in slow motion.'

Then we did some proper acting stuff with our voices. We had to shout out our names in different ways like happily, sadly, angrily, excitedly. Benny seemed to bounce when he was being excited as well as when he was being a football, I noticed. Bouncing Benny. It occurred to me that, actually, Benny is just one big bounce. I said this to him.

He said, 'Boing, boing!'

Anyway, it turns out that drama club won't just be about games and funny business. The games and funny business will help us to be fantastic actors Mrs Parker says, but we're going to be doing this very serious thing as well. We (i.e. the juniors at Holly Hill) are going to be using our magnificent drama skills to help teach the

Boing Boing

little ones (ie the infants) something MEGA important. Road safety! Apparently they're doing a project on it and Mrs Parker says she's written a musical all about it. (I said she was brilliant, didn't I? If Mr Mallory knew I bet he'd be dead jealous. I know he runs choir club but he doesn't write any of the songs.) Then, at the end of term, we're going to perform Mrs Parker's musical at a special infants' road safety day! Isn't that just SO cool? That'll be another day I won't have to spend drawing woodlice.

Benny said, 'I could SO be an actor. I don't know why I haven't thought of it before. Did you see me being a football? I mean, I don't want to boast or anything, but I reckon I'm a natural.'

Paul said, 'Why would anyone boast about being a natural football?'

'No!' said Benny. 'What I mean is, to be able to <u>act</u> being a football, you've got to be able to <u>feel</u> like a football, <u>move</u> like a football, <u>think</u> like a football. And that's what I did.'

'So?' said Sarah. 'That's not such a big deal. After all, maybe you're not just an ordinary boy. Maybe you're part boy, part football.'

'And maybe you're part girl, part sad person,' he said.

And guess what Sarah and I did? We fell about laughing. Like we do.

Bit later

Sarah rang. She sounded all hopeful.

She said, 'Well? Any sign of a letter from Gabby?'

'No,' I said. 'Anyway, why are you ringing? I thought we agreed I'd ring you if a letter had come.'

'We did,' she said. 'I just thought I'd remind you in case you'd forgotten because you were too busy practising thinking like a football or something.'

I said, 'Why would I be practising thinking like a football?'

'Oh, you know,' she said, 'so that you can be a "natural" like Benny. Personally, though, if I've got to learn to act being a "thing", I think I'd rather practise being a hoover.'

'Right,' I said. I didn't ask why. In Sarah's case, sometimes it's best not to know.

At least she didn't sound too disappointed about there being no letter. I was trying not to sound too disappointed either. After all, it would be silly to feel like that, wouldn't it? I don't suppose Gabby's had much time to <u>read</u> our letter yet, let alone to sit down and write one back to us. Besides, not everyone enjoys writing letters. I think most people enjoy reading them but not everyone wants to write them.

Bit later than the last bit

Fortunately for Gabby, I'm the sort of person who loves writing letters. I'm the sort of person who loves writing everything – poems, stories, book reviews for the school mag. Even shopping lists if I'm allowed to include gorgeously delicious shopping like chocolate mousse and lemon drizzle cake. (Naturally I would balance these out with something extremely on the healthy side like strawberries. Only then I suppose I'd have to put squirty cream down as well which would probably mess up the whole healthy strawberry thing. Mmm.)

So, anyway, I thought I'd get down to letter number 2. At least if I keep writing, Gabby'll know I haven't forgotten her – which means that, sooner or later, she'll have to realise that I really do care, whatever she thinks. Besides, I've been thinking that maybe reaching out to Gabby with letters is the best way I can show her God's love. Then one day perhaps she won't be blind anymore …

Dear Gabby,

Yes, it's me again. I just had to write and tell you about drama club. We did it after school today and it was the biggest laugh of all the biggest laughs you've probably ever had. Benny (Topz) was a football. Now he reckons he can think like a football – which, come to think of it, probably explains a lot, but please don't let that put you off coming to stay. He says he wants to be an actor. In fact we all want to be actors now. We're going to be performing this road safety musical for the infants. It might not sound all that exciting to you, but actually it really is. At least it will be when we've rehearsed it, which we're going to be doing every Wednesday after school, and then maybe a few extra times nearer the performance. (Cool – we'll get to miss even more science!) I don't know what part I'm going to play yet but apparently the characters are hedgehogs, cars, lorries and a lollipop person – you know, those people in glowy green jackets outside schools who hold the traffic up for you with a big 'stop' sign so that you can cross the road safely. Oh yes, and there's one double-decker bus in it which Benny wants to play because he says if anyone's going to be able to think like a bus, it's him. (The tragic thing is, he's probably right.) I wish you could come and see our performance. I reckon it's going to be wicked. I'll let you know how rehearsals go.

Hope you got our first letter – the one from Sarah and me. See you, then.

Lots of love Josie XXXXXX

Bedtime

I was talking to Mum about our musical. She says drama is a fantastic way to teach people about things. She says if you can bring something alive by acting it out, it makes it so much more interesting and easy to understand – not just for children, but for grown-ups, too.

And that's got me thinking even more. If we can teach the little kids at school about road safety through drama, why can't we have a Sunday Club drama group to help teach people more about God? Other churches have drama groups. I sometimes see posters up about them. I've just never really thought about why you'd want a drama group in church before. Now I know: to teach people. All the Topz Gang want to be actors so we should DEFINITELY have one. This could be another way to show God's love to people who can't see Him. I'm going to talk to Louise and Greg on Sunday. Tee hee! Sarah is going to SO love this idea!

DRAMA CLUB

In bed

Just think, though! If Gabby came to stay one weekend when our Sunday Club drama group was performing something in church, we'd be able to teach <u>her</u> something about God. We'd be bringing Him alive for her. Just like Mum says.

I don't think I can wait till Sunday to ask Louise about it. I'm ringing her tomorrow.

THURSDAY 25 FEBRUARY

It's very frustrating suddenly coming up with the most

FANDABULOUS

idea in the huge enormousness of the universe and then not being able to tell anyone. Well, I told all the Topz Gang, of course.

I said, 'We've just got to form a Sunday Club drama group,' and they agreed with me that of all the fandabulous ideas we've ever had, this one had to be the most fandabulous since Paul decided to call us the Topz Gang.

But it's Louise and Greg I really need to tell, and I rang Louise but she wasn't in, so I rang Greg and he wasn't in either! Grrrrr!!

Mum said, 'Don't worry. It's Friday tomorrow. You'll be able to see Greg at youth club.'

I said, 'Mum, you just don't get it, do you? This is a fandabulous idea. And fandabulous ideas just have to be talked about.'

Mum said, 'Of course they do. So you can talk about it at youth club tomorrow.'

Urgh! She clearly doesn't have the teeniest clue how much it makes your head want to explode when you know you've been totally brilliant but you can't share your brilliance with the right people. Oh,

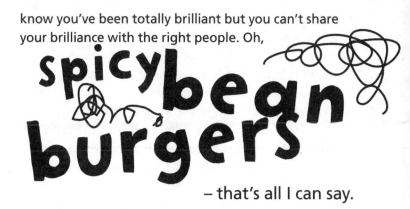

spicy bean burgers

– that's all I can say.

Later
Still no letter from Gabby. Not that I'm really expecting one yet. It takes time to write a letter. Well, not for me, but for other people it probably does.

In bed
Sarah rang.

She said, 'Have you told Louise and Greg about the Sunday Club drama group yet?'

I said, 'No. I've rung them both but they're out. Boring or what?'

She said, 'Oh well, never mind. You can talk to Greg tomorrow.'

I don't believe it. Even Sarah doesn't get the whole head wanting to explode thing.

Sarah said, 'Anyway, I've got a name for us.'

I said, 'What, already?'

She said, 'Well, you can't hang about with these things, you know. When something needs a name, it needs a name. So, if it's all right with you, because after all it is your idea and everything, I thought we could call

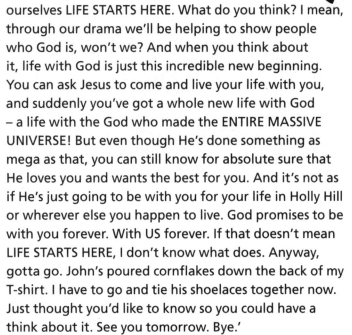

ourselves LIFE STARTS HERE. What do you think? I mean, through our drama we'll be helping to show people who God is, won't we? And when you think about it, life with God is just this incredible new beginning. You can ask Jesus to come and live your life with you, and suddenly you've got a whole new life with God – a life with the God who made the ENTIRE MASSIVE UNIVERSE! But even though He's done something as mega as that, you can still know for absolute sure that He loves you and wants the best for you. And it's not as if He's just going to be with you for your life in Holly Hill or wherever else you happen to live. God promises to be with you forever. With US forever. If that doesn't mean LIFE STARTS HERE, I don't know what does. Anyway, gotta go. John's poured cornflakes down the back of my T-shirt. I have to go and tie his shoelaces together now. Just thought you'd like to know so you could have a think about it. See you tomorrow. Bye.'

Sarah had gone. I was still standing there, holding onto the phone. I didn't say a word. Sarah didn't actually give me a chance to say a word, but I didn't need to anyway. She'd said it all already.

Sometimes, after Sarah's been round here all afternoon and we've been nattering on for hours like we do (with or without the rolling around laughing bit), when she goes home Dad sighs and says, 'Ah! Silence is so golden.' I don't think he's got it right, though. For silence to be golden it has to go with a golden moment. Sarah had just made a moment golden – and I was completely silent.

It's perfect. Her name for us is scarily, spot-on perfect! It says everything. Life starts here …

Thank You, Lord God.

LIFE * STARTS * HERE

FRIDAY 26 FEBRUARY

Had an emergency Topz meeting at break under the climbing frame. Everyone agreed that LIFE STARTS HERE is the coolest name to end all cool names. It's TOPZ being in Topz, that's all I can say!

In fact, today has been a fantasmagorically cool day all round. We spent the afternoon working on our Noah's Ark collage for the blind school. Paul and Dave are in the group doing the ark, but Sarah and I opted for making animals. We're allowed to choose which animals we do, so we had a good rummage through all the materials Mrs Parker had brought in to help us decide. When we saw the plastic tub full of seashells, we both had the same thought. Tortoises! We're going to do one each (as obviously there would have been two of them because the animals went into the ark two by two). There's some rough sort of cloth we can use for their heads and feet, and the seashells will make fantastic tortoise shells. I wanted to know what they would feel like to the blind children, so we spread some of them out on the table and then slid our fingertips over them with our eyes closed. They felt amazing – all hard and nobbly and very ... well ... shell-like.

Paul said, 'What's with all the finger stuff? You look as if you're trying to play a piano that's not there.'

I said, 'Yes, well you would think that, being a boy. But have you ever bothered to <u>feel</u> a seashell before?'

'Er, no,' said Paul. 'Why? Have you?'

'Of course not,' I said 'Well, not until now. I mean, you don't, do you? Not with most things. You don't think about how they feel, you just look at them. But, actually, there's so much more to a thing than how it looks. How it <u>feels</u> is incredible too.'

Mrs Parker says she wants as many contrasting textures on the collage as possible to make it more interesting for the children who will be touching it. So I reckon tortoises and maybe something furry like cats would be a good choice. Someone who shall be nameless (Paul) said that, to make it even more interesting, we could give one of the tortoises a furry shell and a long tail. He said it could be a sort of cross between a cat and a tortoise – called a catoise. Dave seemed to think this was screamingly funny. I just thought, how sad and isn't it odd how some boys have absolutely no idea what's funny and what isn't.

boys!!!!????

After supper

Got to go. Youth Club in a minute. We (that is the Topz Gang) are all going to talk to Greg about our incredible LIFE STARTS HERE drama group. He'll have to go along with it. He won't have a choice. And if by any chance he does seem a bit iffy about it (which he won't, because how could he, but if he does) we can always hide his bike in the girls' toilets.

I thought I might have heard something from Gabby by now. Just a postcard if nothing else. There are lots in her village shop. She could have got one with cows on like I sent to Sarah. You don't have to write much on a postcard. You can just say:

Thanks for your letters. Hope you like this picture of cows in a field in the countryside. We've got lots of them here. Cows, that is. And fields, come to think of it. It also rains a lot.

Lots of love etc, etc XXXXXXXX

You see? Simple. You don't even have to put the kisses. Or the love. You can just put 'from' so you've been polite and answered the other person's letters without making them think you actually care enough about them to want to be their friend.

I'm not annoyed that Gabby hasn't written. Why would you get annoyed about something like that? After all, I only spent the whole of half term with her (almost). If Gabby doesn't want to be my friend, that's fine. I've got more important things to think about than writing letters to her every five minutes now anyway. Much more important things. I'm going to be an actor in a very special drama group with my proper friends. Friends who would definitely take the trouble to write back to me if I took the trouble to write to them.

I feel a bit sorry for Sarah, though. She's the one who's going to be disappointed, not me. I'm not even bothering to look out for a letter any more.

SATURDAY 27 FEBRUARY

Postman's just been. Nothing. Not one single squiddly-diddly thing. Well, that's not quite true. Mum and Dad got a telephone bill.

On the bright side, though, **we've done it!** Topz have done it. We are a definitely formed drama group called LIFE STARTS HERE. It probably won't just be us Topz who are in it, though. Greg says he thinks it would be good for anyone in Sunday Club to join in if they want to, which is fine by us.

When we told Greg about it, he was absolutely bowled over, out and upside down.

He said, 'Well, blow me down! If I was as clever as you lot I might have grown up to be a … clever person.'

Benny said, 'I could act being a clever person, because I'm sure I could think like one.'

Sarah and I looked at him. We didn't say anything, we just looked.

'Of course,' Greg said, 'what you'll have to do now is start thinking about the kind of things you're going to perform. What ideas have you got?'

Ah. Ideas. I suppose that was kind of obvious really. If you're going to form a drama group, you've got to have drama-ish sort of ideas. We just hadn't got round to thinking of any. So far we had a great name but nothing to act.

'Well, you know, stuff,' said Benny. 'We could do a play about the life of Jesus.'

'You could,' said Greg doubtfully, 'but I wonder if that might be a bit ambitious to start with. Why not think about a sketch first of all – a little short scene you can act out in church, like maybe one of the parables Jesus told in the Bible?'

That's actually not a bad idea. And quite drama-ish. If Jesus used parables to teach people about God and how to live life with Him, there's no reason why we can't use them too. Anyway, on Sunday, Greg's going to tell everyone at Sunday Club about LIFE STARTS HERE. Then anyone who wants to be involved can let us know and we can arrange our first 'ideas meeting'. Snazzy, eh?

Before lunch
Sarah rang.

She said, 'Well?'
I said, 'What?'
She said, 'Anything?'
I said, 'Huh?'
She said, 'Post!'
I said, 'Oh. No.'
And that was it, really.

After lunch

Mum said, 'You're upset about Gabby, aren't you?'

I said, 'Why would I be upset about Gabby? It's not as if I'm ever going to see her again.'

'I don't think that's true,' said Mum. 'After all, she's one of the family now.'

'Try telling that to her,' I said.

'Maybe she's not very good at writing letters.'

'I don't care. I've tried to be friends. She's not interested. It's fine.'

'But she hasn't even had your letters for a week,' Mum said. 'Just because she hasn't written back straight-away doesn't mean she's not going to write back at all.'

'I don't care,' I said again. 'I've given up with her.'

Later

Mum came into my room. She was so surprised she had to sit down. I've tidied it up.

'Am I in the right house?' she said.

Oh, ha ha.

Then she said, 'Please don't give up with Gabby. Of all the people you know, she's probably the one who most needs you to be her friend.'

'No, she doesn't,' I said. 'She doesn't want friends. She said so.'

Mum said, 'I know it's frustrating. You keep trying to reach out to her and you get nothing back. But imagine what it's like for God. Think of all the people He's trying to reach out to who go on refusing to have anything to do with Him. He doesn't give up on us, though. He can't. He loves us all too much and He wants all of us to have the chance of a life with Him.'

'But I tried to tell Gabby about God,' I said. 'I tried to

let her know how special she is to Him. And Uncle Rich and Auntie Chrissie must have told her loads of times. Gabby won't even go to church with them.'

'Things don't always happen as quickly as we want them to,' Mum said.

'In Gabby's case, they're not going to happen at all.'

'You don't know that. Gabby's had a very different life from you. She's been let down and disappointed by some important people. She probably doesn't know <u>how</u> to trust someone, let alone <u>who</u> to trust. What you've got to do is keep reaching out. And if in the end Gabby still won't let you be a proper friend, at least you'll know that you've been the kind of person God wants you to be. You'll have tried to help someone, not for what you'll get out of it, but simply because that person needs your help.'

'But it's easy for you,' I said. 'You're that sort of reaching out person already. You're always doing stuff for people, being kind, helping them.'

'That doesn't mean I always feel like it,' she laughed. 'You'd be amazed. Sometimes being the person God wants me to be is <u>so</u> hard and <u>so</u> not what I feel like being that I really struggle with it. I have to say to Him, "Lord, I cannot do this, but I know You can. Please be with me and shine through me. I need Your love to help me love other people today."'

I suppose that means I need God's love to help me love Gabby right now. I mean, Christians can't give up, can they? People need to see God's love in us all the time to help them realise that it doesn't just stop one day but goes on and on. Mum's love goes on and on, too. She's special, my mum. I don't know if I'll ever be able to be as special as she is. I've got to give it a go though.

love goes on and on and on and on and on and on and on and on and on and on and on and on

Dear Gabby,

I know what you're thinking – oh please, no, not another letter! I suppose I can be a bit annoying when it comes to writing letters. I do tend to go on quite a lot when I've got someone to write to. It probably comes from being such a chatty person. There's always something happening I want to yabber on about. So, sorry to keep pestering you, but if you want me to stop writing, you'll have to write back and tell me, otherwise I shall just keep going. After all, when you've got to write, you've got to write, if you know what I mean.

So, what are you up to? I'm about to be so busy I shall soon know what it's like to be an incredibly busy person. If all this had happened before half term, I probably wouldn't have had time to come and stay. I told you about the school drama club. Well, now we're forming another one in church at Sunday Club. Only as we haven't got Mrs Parker there giving us crazy musicals about road safety to work on, we've got to come up with all our own stuff. So, not only have I got to be an actor, I've got to be a writing sort of person as well. You may think that shouldn't be a problem for someone like me who spends most of her time writing in her diary and writing letters. But writing stuff to act in front of an audience is totally different. It's got to make sense for a start. I mean, because we want to teach people about God through what we act, they've got to be able to understand what we're on about. Hopefully we'll be performing in church very soon. I'll let you know when.

Then, if you're thinking of coming up for a visit, you could come when we're doing our performance, and you might learn a bit more about God. After all, the more you get to know Him and spend time with Him, the more you'll realise He won't let you down and the easier it'll be to let Him share your life.

Better get some sleep now, I suppose, although actually I feel as if I could yabber away all night. (Don't worry, I'm not going to.)

Love from Josie XXXXXXXXX

P.S. I might take this letter to Sunday Club tomorrow to see if Sarah wants to add a bit. She's even more chatty than I am. (I know. Hard to believe.) J

SUNDAY 28 FEBRUARY

LIFE STARTS HERE is launched! Now we are not only definitely formed, we are a 'happening' drama group! People are going to be turning up from all over the entire whole enormous world to see us perform (possibly). We've got it! We know what we're going to act and we might even be going to act it in church

NEXT SUNDAY!!

It's all down to Louise and what she was doing with us at Sunday Club.

She said, 'Who remembers the story Jesus told about the wise and foolish builders?'

I think all of us put our hands up. It's an easy one

to remember because there's a song we sing about it with actions, so we know it pretty well. It's a very clever story, too, I always think. Jesus explains that if we listen to Him and try to live the way God wants us to, we're like a wise man who builds his house on solid rock – when the storms and floods come, the house doesn't fall down because it's built on a strong foundation. It can't be washed away. What Jesus means is that, if we build our lives on God by reading the Bible, trying to do the things He wants us to do, praying and listening to Him, then He will hang onto us and hold us up no matter what happens. And, in the end, we'll be able to be with Him forever.

But if we decide to live our lives WITHOUT Him, and take no notice of Him or what He tries to teach us through the Bible, then we're like a foolish man who builds his house on sand. When the storms come, that

house is washed away in no time like a sandcastle on the beach when the tide comes in. One big wave and it's all over. Without the solid rock foundation, we have nothing to hold us up because we don't have God to guide us and look after us. So instead of being <u>with</u> God forever, we'll have to live <u>without</u> Him forever and all because we just won't listen to Him and live the way He wants us to NOW.

'It's like the name for your new drama group,' Louise said unexpectedly. (Well, <u>I</u> certainly wasn't expecting her to bring us into it.) 'Life starts HERE. Not this evening, or tomorrow, or even next week, but right here and now. You see, God's not floating up in the sky somewhere out of reach and, maybe if we're lucky He might drop in on us sometime before He shoots off again. God's here NOW. He's ready for us NOW. So we need to live for Him here and now.'

Isn't Louise brilliant – I mean really, crazily, mouth-gapingly brilliant? In fact I think she should definitely be a co-member of LIFE STARTS HERE because then we can all be brilliant together! As usual, she managed to say exactly the right thing at exactly the right time (with quite a lot of help from Jesus' clever parable, of course). So obviously that's when it happened. All the LIFE STARTS HERE lot had exactly the same idea at pretty well exactly the same time: the story of the wise and foolish builders could be our first drama sketch! We all started looking at each other and putting our hands up and fidgeting about, just like you do at school when you really, really want to say something but you know you've got to wait because you're not supposed to butt in and interrupt the teacher. Louise didn't make us wait as long as Mrs Parker does, though.

'Whatever's all this? Is it something I said?' she asked.

'Well ... yes, actually!' we all exploded.

There was still a while to go before Sunday Club ended, so Louise said that whoever wanted to be involved in the drama could spend the time working on some ideas together, and anyone who didn't could do some artwork with her based on the story.

There were nine of us in the end for LIFE STARTS HERE – all the Topz Gang plus Eddie and Rhianna.

Benny said, 'OK. Who's going to play what?'

Danny said, 'Don't we need to work out what the parts are first?'

Benny said, 'Oh yeah. Great idea. Can I be the rock? I'd make a really terrific rock.'

Sarah and I looked at each other.

'Um ... how can you be a rock?' I said.

'Don't you know anything about acting?' said Benny.

'Like this.'

Then he curled up on the floor with his head down and his back facing upwards. To be honest, he looked more like a hibernating tortoise than a rock but I didn't say so. Why spoil it for him?

'Right,' I said. 'So … now what?'

'So,' said Benny, lifting his head up so that he looked more like a tortoise waking up from hibernation and even less like a rock, 'whoever's going to be the house on the rock has to stand on my back.'

'I could do that,' said Paul. He was jumping around very excitedly. Quite worryingly so, in fact. 'I'll be the perfect house. I've got glasses and everything. They can be the windows!'

Next minute he was standing on Benny's back holding his arms over his head in a sort of upside down V-shape like a roof.

'What do you think?' he said. 'Mega convincing, or what?'

'Mega convincing,' everyone agreed, just before Paul fell off Benny who decided to stand up without warning him first.

That obviously gave Eddie an idea because suddenly it was his turn to get excited.

'Ooh, ooh!' he said, hopping about. 'If Benny's going to be the rock, can I be the sand? Then, when the storm comes, I can wriggle about and knock the house of my back.'

'Wicked!' said Benny. 'You're getting into this like me. You're <u>thinking</u> like sand.'

I must say, I do sometimes wonder what boys' brains are made of. But, having said that, they were coming up with some pretty cool ideas, so who am I to argue with someone who can think like a rock?

By the end of Sunday Club, we had it all sorted, as follows:

LIFE STARTS HERE
PRESENTS:

How To Build A House That Lasts

(That's the title Sarah came up with. She may not be able to think like a rock but everyone agrees she is VERY spectacular with words.)

Starring:

SARAH as the wise man (Who else could it possibly be after her incredibly wise, not to mention brainy, sketch title?)

ME as the foolish man (It's OK, I don't mind. Honestly.)

RHIANNA as the narrator (We thought it would be a good idea to have someone telling the story while we acted it out, just in case anyone didn't quite get the whole Benny and Eddie being the rock and the sand thing.)

Benny as the rock (Or the tortoise, depending on how you look at life.)

EDDIE as the sand.

PAUL as the house on the rock (with windows).

DANNY as the house on the sand. (Obvious choice as he's very sporty and will be able to do a spectacular fall.)

DAVE as the wind. (He reckons he's got good lungs and will be able to blow at us like a hurricane. Nice.)

JOHN as the rain. (We thought it would be funny if the person playing the rain squirted water at us, and John said if anyone was going to squirt water at Sarah, it was him. Sarah said it was fine and she'd get him back when he was least expecting it with something far worse than water.)

Louise was very impressed. She said any kind of drama project has to be a real team effort for it to work and we were obviously a real team already. Of course we still need to get a script together, but she says that, now we've got a story and know what all the parts are, we'll be able to work the rest out as we go along. She's going to come down to church tomorrow evening and help us with our first proper rehearsal, and if it goes really well, she says she'll see whether we can perform it next

Sunday. So, as well as tomorrow, we've arranged to practise at youth club on Friday and we can meet next Saturday morning as well. Groovy, eh? Being an actor is just so cool!

I said to Louise just before I went home, 'I'm so glad you did that story today. I don't suppose we'd ever have thought of it on our own. It's perfect for LIFE STARTS HERE, isn't it? I mean we'll be showing people that life starts with building your life on God.'

I noticed she had a sort of cheeky smile on her face, which freaked me out a bit because, although she's definitely quite zany and funny, I'd never had her down as a cheeky smiley kind of person.

'What?' I said.

'Plant a seed and watch it grow,' she answered. Then she winked at me. Yes, she WINKED at me. Huh?

I was halfway home before it finally clicked. Greg must have told Louise about our drama group and the fact that we needed a sketch. She obviously thought the story of the wise and foolish builders would be a good one for us to start with so, without our realising it, she deliberately gave us the idea (planted the seed in other words). Grown-ups can be clever sometimes. Sneaky but very clever.

After supper

I was also halfway home when I realised I hadn't asked Sarah if she wanted to add anything to my letter to Gabby. When I rang her up to see she said, 'Do I ever!' so Mum said I could go round to her house this afternoon. Sarah wrote (in her instantly recognisable, funky capitals, of course):

HI GABBY. WE'VE JUST HAD THE MOST WOWZY DAY. NOT ONLY ARE WE GOING TO BE WORLD FAMOUS ACTORS AFTER NEXT SUNDAY WHEN WE PERFORM OUR TOTALLY AMAZING DRAMA SKETCH IN CHURCH (IF YOU WANT TO KNOW MORE, YOU'LL JUST HAVE TO COME AND SEE IT), BUT ALSO WE HAD APPLE CRUMBLE AND CUSTARD FOR PUDDING AT LUNCHTIME – <u>AND</u> THERE'S A TINY BIT LEFT OVER FOR LATER! I THINK JOHN WANTS IT (FOR INFO ON JOHN, PLEASE REFER TO MY CHARACTER PROFILE IF YOU STILL HAVE IT), BUT HE'S GOING TO GET TO SQUIRT ME WITH WATER NEXT WEEK, SO I RECKON I DESERVE IT MORE THAN HE DOES.

IN CASE YOU'RE NOT SURE WHETHER TO COME AND SEE OUR FANDABBY DRAMA SKETCH, HERE'S SOMETHING TO HELP YOU MAKE UP YOUR MIND – A SNEAK PREVIEW OF JUST HOW WICKED IT'S ACTUALLY GOING TO BE. HONESTLY, IT'S A REAL 'MUST SEE'!

For the inside story on how to build a house that lasts, come and watch the master builders at work next Sunday!

(This is where we drew a picture of us all doing the <u>How To Build A House That Lasts</u> sketch. The two houses (Paul and Danny) are standing on Benny and Eddie (the rock and the sand). Sarah and me, we're standing by our houses. Dave is blowing at us madly with an enormous fat face and John is wearing a huge grin and squirting water everywhere out of a hosepipe. Obviously when we actually do the sketch on Sunday he won't have a hosepipe. He'll probably have a washing-up liquid bottle, but a hosepipe looked funnier for the picture. Then we drew Rhianna's face saying: For the inside story on how to build a house that lasts, come and watch the master builders at work next Sunday!)

Geniuses. That's what we are, Sarah and me. Pure geniuses. (Is it geniuses or genii? Or is that something that flew out of a lamp in <u>Aladdin</u>?) Oh well, who cares? Whatever it is, even Gabby will have to admit that, as pictures go, this one is dead brilliant (probably).

When we'd finished, I noticed that Sarah was getting that goggly-eyed look that happens when she has an excited thought about something.

'Maybe,' she squealed (squealing's something else that happens when Sarah has an excited thought about something), 'maybe Gabby will draw a picture for us, too. I mean, if she's finding it hard to write a letter, maybe that's what she'll do instead.'

For a moment her eyes got even gogglier.

Then, 'For instance,' she squealed, 'she might do a picture of herself sitting in her tree house.'

'I don't think so,' I said, feeling a bit mean about

having to ungoggle Sarah's eyes. 'It's just that, Gabby doesn't draw people or places or things that have anything to do with her life. She says all that stuff's private and nothing to do with anyone else. She only ever does patterns. She says the patterns are all about her feelings but no one will ever understand what she's painted. She likes that, you see, keeping everything to herself, making sure no one else knows anything.'

'Oh,' said Sarah, frowning. 'Still, she could draw a made-up person.'

'When I was there, she wouldn't even draw a cow,' I said.

'Oh,' said Sarah. 'Well, maybe she'll just send us a pattern, then.'

'Maybe,' I said.

I said 'Maybe', but that's not what I thought. What I thought was, I doubt Gabby's going to send us anything at all.

Going to bed

All right, so I admit that this is quite early to bed for me. It's only 8.00pm. But I've decided, if you're going to be an incredibly busy person, then you're going to need extra sleep to make up for your incredible busyness.

So I said to Mum, 'I'm going to bed now.'

She said, 'I'm sorry, I think I must be hearing things. I'm sure you just said you were going to bed.'

'I did,' I said patiently. 'Busy people need extra sleep and, in case you hadn't noticed, I am an incredibly busy person now.'

I said to Dad, 'Night, night, Dad.'

He pretended to fall off the sofa.

He said, 'You? Going to bed? Now? Is it me or has my watch stopped?'

I didn't bother to answer. Sometimes silence can be more crushing than a thousand words.

MONDAY 1 MARCH

Can't stop long. Got to get ready for our first proper LIFE STARTS HERE rehearsal. I am SO excited. In fact, being this excited all day long and still having to pretend to care what happens to the decimal point when you multiply a number by 100 has taken quite a huge amount of effort on my part. Not that Mrs Parker appreciated it. She said, if I couldn't keep my mind on what I was supposed to be doing, could I at least hold my legs still and stop jiggling my knees. I mean, can I help it if my knees jiggle when I get excited? Sarah's eyes go goggly and I've got jiggly knees. That's just the way it is …
And, I'm sorry, but decimals are head-achingly boring.

Rhianna is just a total superstar, though. She's only gone and written the wise and foolish builder story already so that it's all sorted for tonight.

'I thought I might as well,' she said when she showed it to us at lunchtime, as if all she'd done was something amazingly UNimportant, like move an ant from one side of a leaf to the other. 'After all, I'm the one who's got to read it.'

It's fantastic, too, what she's written. Everyone's going to go mad for it. It starts like this:

> Once upon a time, there was a rock. It was a good rock. A solid rock. The sort of rock that would never let you down if you built your house upon it. And once upon the same time, there was also some sand. It was beautiful and golden. But sand can be tricky. It doesn't always hold together the way you'd like it to, and when it comes to building houses, it's definitely NOT a good foundation.

I mean, isn't that just an absolutely whiz-the-biz way to begin?! Benny was dead happy because, being the rock, he says he gets to be the first person to act in the sketch. I pointed out that Rhianna is really the first person to act in the sketch because she actually starts it off by narrating the story.

Only then Benny said, 'Yes, but narrating isn't quite the same as actual acting, is it? I mean, don't get me wrong, it's a really important job and everything, but it's reading not acting. That's why when you narrate a

story you're called a narrator. If narrators were actors they wouldn't be called narrators, would they?'

'Right,' I said, 'thanks for that, Benny.' That's about all I could say, really.

Bedtime

Brilliant rehearsal. Although I do feel there's just a slight chance Benny might possibly be taking this thinking like a rock thing a little too far.

He said, 'How about if the rock has a name?'

'What do you mean?' asked Rhianna.

'Well,' said Benny, 'I've got to act like a rock, haven't I? If I had a rock-like name, it might help me to get more into the character.'

'Benny,' said Rhianna kindly, 'you're just a rock. Rocks don't have names.'

'I know they don't, normally,' he said, 'but we're acting, aren't we? We can do what we want. I could be called something like ...'

'Rocky?' suggested Paul helpfully.

'Yeah!' said Benny. 'Once upon a time there was a rock called Rocky. Stonking! You see? We can build it into the story. We can bring this rock alive.'

I'm glad Louise was there.

She said, 'Um, Benny, what we're trying to bring alive is Jesus' words. I think the rock should just be a rock, don't you?'

When we went home, Benny had started on about his costume. He wants to have tufts of grass. He says you get that sometimes with rocks.

TUESDAY 2 MARCH — NEARLY BEDTIME ALREADY

Being incredibly busy and trying to go to bed early really cuts down your writing time. It wouldn't have been so bad only Mrs Parker is giving us a decimals test tomorrow morning so I had to work my way through this duller-than-dullest revision sheet.

I rang Sarah.

I said, 'Have you done it?'

She said, 'Have I done what?'

I said, 'Your revision sheet.'

'Not yet,' she said. 'I thought I'd learn my wise man's lines first since Louise says we're definitely performing on Sunday.'

'Oh,' I said. 'I thought I'd do it the other way round. Dull stuff first than learn my lines.'

'Right,' she said. 'How's it going?'

'Dull,' I said. '**Dull**, **duller** and **dullest.**

In that order. With or without the decimal point.'

Bedtime

I was thinking about Gabby earlier and wishing she could come and see our sketch in church. I prayed,

> Dear God, I don't know what Gabby's been up to since half term, not having heard a word from her, but I know that You know. However much she wants to hide away from me, she can't hide away from You. Please help her to understand one day that You can be the rock in her life because You'll never leave her. And I hope she liked our drawing. Amen.

By the way, Mrs Parker's sorted out the parts for the road safety musical. Sarah and I are going to be hedgehogs. And, yes. Benny does get to be the double-decker bus.

WEDNESDAY 3 MARCH

Got back from school after drama club and Mum called through from the kitchen, 'I've got something for you and I think you're going to like it.'

I sniffed. Usually when she says things like that it means she's been baking chocolate brownies. You know it the minute you walk in the door because of the gorgeous smell. There was nothing today, though. Except just a faint whiff of peach blossom air freshener.

'What?' I said.

'This,' she answered.

And there it was. A letter. Well, I assumed it must be a letter. It was something in an envelope and it was addressed to me.

I stared at it. I didn't take hold of it or anything, I just stared.

'Is it ...' I said, 'is it from Gabby?'

'It is,' said Mum.

'Really?' I said.

'Really,' she said.

'Are you sure?' I said.

'I mean, it <u>could be</u> from someone else, couldn't it?'

'It could,' she said. 'But I think the fact that she's written

"Strictly private – from Gabby"

on the back of the envelope is a bit of a giveaway, don't you?'

I grabbed it and tore it open.

There was one sheet of paper inside. Along the top, Gabby had written:

Dear Josie and Sarah,

Thank you for your letters. You're obviously both completely crazy. I'm not very good at writing letters myself, so, as you also drew me a picture, I thought I'd draw one for you. Here it is.

And there it was. It wasn't a pattern. It was a proper picture. And it wasn't a picture of a cow or a tree or even a tree house. It was a picture of Gabby herself, but she wasn't on her own. On one side, she'd drawn me, grinning away like an idiot, with 'Josie' written on my T-shirt, and on the other she'd drawn a picture of Sarah. Gabby must have copied it from the photo on Sarah's character profile because she'd drawn her wearing her cycle helmet.

Underneath the picture, Gabby had written in different coloured capital letters:

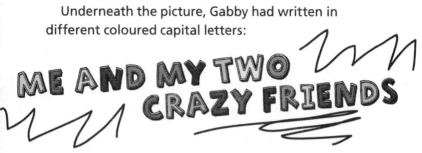

ME AND MY TWO CRAZY FRIENDS

There was nothing else. No news. No chat. She just signed off after that:

Love Gabby (short for Gabriella, which my dad told me was my mum's favourite name. But that's my biggest secret so don't you dare tell anyone.) XX

I must have gone dead quiet. Gabby had managed to say more on her one small sheet of paper than I could ever say in a million letters. Mum came over and put her arm round me.

'Everything all right?' she said.

I couldn't speak. I just nodded.

All right? It was more than all right. It was more than more than **MORE THAN ALL RIGHT!**

Gabby doesn't draw people or anything to do with her life, but she'd drawn a picture of the three of us. Gabby doesn't let anyone in, but she'd called Sarah and me her friends. Gabby doesn't share her secrets but she'd shared her biggest secret when she signed her name.

We'd reached out to her, Sarah and me. We hadn't given up because God doesn't give up. We'd tried as hard as we could to show her His love.

And at last Gabby was reaching back to us.

All right? How could anything NOT be all right ever again?

Thank You, Lord God. Thank You, thank You, oh

Collect the set:

IF YOU LIKED THIS BOOK, YOU'LL LOVE THESE:

TOPZ

An exciting, day-by-day look at the Bible for children aged from 7 to 11. As well as simple prayers and Bible readings every day, each issue includes word games, puzzles, cartoons and contributions from readers. Fun and colourful, *Topz* helps children get to know God.
ISSN: 0967-1307
£2.49 each (bimonthly, plus p&p)
£13.80 UK annual subscription
(bimonthly, p&p included in UK)

TOPZ FOR NEW CHRISTIANS

Thirty days of Bible notes to help 7- to 11- year-olds find faith in Jesus and have fun exploring their new life with Him.
ISBN: 978-1-85345-104-1
£2.49

TOPZ GUIDE TO THE BIBLE

A guide offering exciting and stimulating ways for 7- to 11- year-olds to become familiar with God's Word. With a blend of colourful illustrations, cartoons and lively writing, this is the perfect way to encourage children to get to know their Bibles.
ISBN: 978-1-85345-313-7
£2.99

National Distributors

UK: (and countries not listed below)
CWR, Waverley Abbey House, Waverley Lane, Farnham, Surrey GU9 8EP.
Tel: (01252) 784700 Outside UK (44) 1252 784700 Email: mail@cwr.org.uk

AUSTRALIA: KI Entertainment, Unit 21 317-321 Woodpark Road, Smithfield,
New South Wales 2164. Tel: 1 800 850 777 Fax: 02 9604 3699
Email: sales@kientertainment.com.au

CANADA: David C Cook Distribution Canada, PO Box 98, 55 Woodslee Avenue,
Paris, Ontario N3L 3E5 Tel: 1800 263 2664 Email: swansons@cook.ca

GHANA: Challenge Enterprises of Ghana, PO Box 5723, Accra.
Tel: (021) 222437/223249 Fax: (021) 226227 Email: ceg@africaonline.com.gh

HONG KONG: Cross Communications Ltd, 1/F, 562A Nathan Road, Kowloon.
Tel: 2780 1188 Fax: 2770 6229 Email: cross@crosshk.com

INDIA: Crystal Communications, 10-3-18/4/1, East Marredpalli,
Secunderabad – 500026, Andhra Pradesh. Tel/Fax: (040) 27737145
Email: crystal_edwj@rediffmail.com

KENYA: Keswick Books and Gifts Ltd, PO Box 10242-00400, Nairobi.
Tel: (254) 20 312639/3870125 Email: keswick@swiftkenya.com

MALAYSIA: Canaanland, No. 25 Jalan PJU 1A/41B, NZX Commercial Centre,
Ara Jaya, 47301 Petaling Jaya, Selangor. Tel: (03) 7885 0540/1/2
Fax: (03) 7885 0545 Email: info@canaanland.com.my
Salvation Book Centre (M) Sdn Bhd, 23 Jalan SS 2/64, 47300 Petaling Jaya,
Selangor. Tel: (03) 78766411/78766797 Fax: (03) 78757066/78756360
Email: info@salvationbookcentre.com

NEW ZEALAND: KI Entertainment, Unit 21 317-321 Woodpark Road,
Smithfield, New South Wales 2164, Australia. Tel: 0 800 850 777
Fax: +612 9604 3699 Email: sales@kientertainment.com.au

NIGERIA: FBFM, Helen Baugh House, 96 St Finbarr's College Road, Akoka,
Lagos. Tel: (01) 7747429/4700218/825775/827264 Email: fbfm@hyperia.com

PHILIPPINES: OMF Literature Inc, 776 Boni Avenue, Mandaluyong City.
Tel: (02) 531 2183 Fax: (02) 531 1960 Email: gloadlaon@omflit.com

SINGAPORE: Alby Commercial Enterprises Pte Ltd, 95 Kallang Avenue #04-00,
AIS Industrial Building, 339420. Tel: (65) 629 27238 Fax: (65) 629 27235
Email: marketing@alby.com.sg

SOUTH AFRICA: Struik Christian Books, 80 MacKenzie Street, PO Box 1144,
Cape Town 8000. Tel: (021) 462 4360 Fax: (021) 461 3612
Email: info@struikchristianmedia.co.za

SRI LANKA: Christombu Publications (Pvt) Ltd, Bartleet House,
65 Braybrooke Place, Colombo 2. Tel: (9411) 2421073/2447665
Email: dhanad@bartleet.com

USA: David C Cook Distribution Canada, PO Box 98, 55 Woodslee Avenue,
Paris, Ontario N3L 3E5, Canada. Tel: 1800 263 2664 Email: swansons@cook.ca

CWR is a Registered Charity – Number 294387
CWR is a Limited Company registered in England – Registration Number 1990308